RELUCTANT LOVE

Frankie Green worked happily as an electronics engineer for her grandfather's firm, Pickard's. Then, into her life came Paul Hillwood, who worked in the sales department of Pickard's biggest customer. He asked Frankie if she could accompany him to Istanbul for a few days to try to persuade a Turkish company to buy machinery from them. Frankie and Paul seemed to have disliked each other on sight, but in Turkey they began to realise feelings could change . . .

SHEILA HOLROYD

◆

RELUCTANT LOVE

Complete and Unabridged

LINFORD
Leicester

First published in Great Britain in 2000

First Linford Edition
published 2001

British Library CIP Data

Holroyd, Sheila
    Reluctant love.—Large print ed.—
Linford romance library
1. Love stories
2. Large type books
I. Title
823.9'14 [F]

ISBN 0–7089–9757–0

Published by
F. A. Thorpe (Publishing)
Anstey, Leicestershire

Set by Words & Graphics Ltd.
Anstey, Leicestershire
Printed and bound in Great Britain by
T. J. International Ltd., Padstow, Cornwall

This book is printed on acid-free paper

1

Frankie was underneath the old car, happily engaged in trying to solve the suspension problems of the forty-year-old vehicle, and grimaced with annoyance at the sound of a car drawing up. A visitor was an unwanted distraction at this critical moment. A car door was shut firmly and brisk, confident foot-steps strode up the concrete drive and stopped by the side of the dilapidated coupé. Frankie felt a sharp tap on the sole of one of the working boots that protruded from under the car.

'Hey, you!' an imperious voice came.

Frankie sighed and slid out from under the chassis. A tall, dark man in an elegant business suit looked down impatiently.

'I'm looking for Miss Green. I was told this was her cottage.'

Frankie stood up reluctantly, wiping

1

dirty hands down the sides of oil-stained overalls, and pulled off the knitted, woollen cap. Bright gold hair tumbled to her shoulders.

'I am Miss Green. Can I help you?' she said matter-of-factly.

She waited patiently for the new-comer to digest the fact that the dirty, untidy figure facing him was a girl in her mid-twenties. For some reason, the discovery of her femininity produced not only the astonishment that might have been expected in this man, but he seemed ready to be annoyed and even angry. The fact that she was a woman was somehow an unwelcome shock to him.

'Are you sure?'

Frankie looked back at him in silence and he reddened, aware of the stupidity of this remark. He obviously did not like his dignity to suffer.

'I'm sorry, but you are not what I was expecting. I was sent to look for a Frances Green. Nobody told me that it was the feminine Frances!'

And whoever had neglected to tell him that would be in trouble soon, his tone indicated. She shrugged carelessly.

'You're not the first person to make the mistake when they've found me working on the car. Everybody calls me Frankie anyway.'

Dropping the subject, she looked at him enquiringly.

'Who sent you anyway and why?'

'My name is Paul Hillwood. I'm here on business about your work that will take some time to explain. I need to talk to you now.'

He looked up at the bleak, Yorkshire sky, threatening October rain. Frankie looked across to the next garden where a tall, fair-haired man was digging up a flower-bed.

'A visitor from the factory, John,' she called across.

The gardener stared at the smartly-dressed man and nodded briefly, as Frankie led the way into the interior of the small, stone cottage. She was aware that his swift glance was noting the

3

basic nature of the furnishings, the comfortable but shabby suite and the faded curtains which she had been meaning to change ever since she had moved in two years ago. His gaze rested briefly on the abandoned plate of baked beans that had been her snack lunch! She picked up the plate.

'If you'd like to sit down I'll put on the kettle.'

'Please, don't bother. I'm not thirsty,' he replied.

'But I am,' she said crisply, going through to the small kitchen and leaving him to perch on one of the upright dining chairs which were the only seating apart from the large couch and an old rocking-chair which he clearly considered beneath his dignity.

She reflected that he would have been surprised by the contrast of the kitchen and sitting-room. Although space was limited, the gleaming kitchen was expertly fitted to make good use of every inch, and displayed all the latest culinary gadgets. Frankie was a good cook when she felt like it and happily settled for baked beans when she didn't. Rapidly she stripped off the overalls and washed her hands, peered in the small wall mirror and rubbed impatiently at the streak of grease which marked one cheek.

When she carried the tea tray into the sitting-room five minutes later, she saw the tall figure of her visitor outlined against the light from the big, single-paned window that occupied most of the back view.

'You have a magnificent view,' he commented. 'It's always surprising to find such beautiful country so near an industrial town like Bradford.'

Her grey eyes clouded.

'That sounds as if you come from the South. Did you expect to find the whole of Yorkshire still covered in smoke and coal mines?'

A flicker of impatience at this reaction crossed his face as he came forward and took the tray from her.

'I may come from London but I

wasn't being patronising. I was simply stating a fact.'

Without being asked, he set the tea things out on the small table and took his seat on one side, leaving her to sit opposite him. She realised that he had automatically turned the encounter into a business meeting.

Sitting facing him as she sipped her tea, she eyed him covertly as he pushed his cup aside and took various papers from his briefcase. His short, dark hair was thick enough to resist his efforts to comb it tidily flat, but otherwise the perfectly-cut suit, pristine white shirt and silk tie fitted the image of the successful business man, probably about ten years older than she was. He looked up suddenly and she was aware of hollows under the high cheekbones of his lean face, and the dark shadows of weariness under his dark eyes.

'As I told you, I'm Paul Hillwood,' he told her. 'Incidentally, I'm sorry to disturb you on a Sunday, but this is urgent.'

She nodded calmly and waited for him to continue.

'I work in the sales department of LRT Limited. As you know, we are probably your firm's biggest customers, and we use a lot of your products in the machine tools we make. We've been particularly impressed by some of the new developments you have produced recently, much more innovative than anything Pickard's has done before. They've been quite surprising for such a small firm.'

He saw her face tighten, and lifted a hand deprecatingly.

'Once again, I'm not being patronising. Successful research and development means either a lot of money or someone very talented, and usually both. We made enquiries, and found that most of the news ideas at Pickard's seemed to be originating with a certain F. Green, though I assume there must be capable assistants.'

He stopped as he saw her face set grimly.

'So now you've found out you've come to offer me a job with your firm!' she exclaimed. 'That's why you've come to see me here, I suppose, instead of waiting to see me at the factory. Well, you're wasting your time. You are not the first person who's tried to get me away from Pickard's, but I'm happy there and I'm staying there,' she finished hotly.

His look was icily reproving.

'You keep jumping to conclusions, Miss Green. Why not listen to me first? You are quite wrong, as it happens. You are producing what we want where you are. We don't want to disrupt a winning team.'

She realised that his response was justified and bit her lip as she looked down at the table, reluctant to apologise in the face of his arrogance.

'What do you want then? What is so urgent that you've had to come searching for me at the week-end?'

'Early on Tuesday I'm flying from Manchester to Istanbul for a very

8

important sales mission. I found that I needed more information before I went so I came to see this F. Green.'

He hesitated before he spoke again.

'I want you to come with me.'

She gaped across at him, utterly dumbfounded.

'What? Istanbul? With you? Why?'

He lifted an eyebrow with careful patience.

'Once again, I will explain, if you listen.'

He pushed the papers in front of him aside and leaned forward urgently.

'Turkey is a very important market. Europe and Asia meet there, and if we can persuade the firm in Istanbul to use our machine tools it will not only be a big order but it may be a breakthrough that will open up new markets. Now, the equipment they are interested in incorporates some of the latest electronic devices. I can sell the tools, I know all about them, but I have decided that just asking you a few questions isn't enough. I need an expert with me to explain those devices. The designer seems the logical choice.'

He stopped, and Frankie looked at him wryly.

'But you expected me to be a man.'

For the first time, he smiled, a brief gleam that lit up his face.

'Yes, I admit that was the assumption. And don't jump to the conclusion that I'm anti-feminist or don't think girls can do it. It's just a fact that there are very few female electronic engineers.'

Of course he was right. In Pickard's, in the world of electronic engineers, Frankie was accepted, her work appreciated, as was shown by the other firms that had approached her, but time and again outside the factory she had encountered amazement that an attractive girl of twenty-five could be a successful electronic engineer.

'I suppose the discovery that I'm Frances, female version, means you don't really want me to come to Istanbul,' she said a little wistfully.

His hesitation showed again momentarily before he shrugged.

'Why not? This is a business trip. I admit a woman might not have been my first choice, but we'd be working together, that's all.'

His cool gaze weighed up the faded sweatshirt that she had been wearing with her old jeans under the dirty overalls and he frowned slightly.

'I admit you don't look as if you would fit into a business meeting at the moment.'

She met his gaze with equal coolness.

'I don't wear my best clothes to mend cars, but I assure you I can look businesslike when I choose to. However, that's a minor matter. LRT may want me to go to Istanbul, but Pickard's would have to approve of my going, and I'm not sure they would do that.'

'My directors contacted old Pickard yesterday evening and he gave them permission for me to contact you. After all, sales for LRT mean sales for

Pickard's. Any other difficulties?'

She considered her answer carefully before replying.

'I admit I would like to go to Istanbul. One difficulty of working in a small firm and selling our products through other firms is that we don't get enough feedback from the ultimate customer, and that could be valuable. But there is one major difficulty still, I'm afraid.'

'What is it? Perhaps I can see a way to solve the problem. If it's a matter of money, or is there a boyfriend who'll object to you going off with me?'

She was shaking her head.

'Nothing like that. It's simply that I've never flown before.'

He stared at her in astonishment.

'Never flown? Do you mean you've never left this country? Haven't you ever been on a package holiday? Oh, no, and are you saying you haven't got a passport?'

Her laugh was a little shaky,

'Relax. I have got a passport because

I go to France every summer. But I've always gone by car and ferry. However, I've never been on an aeroplane and I've never planned to go on one. For certain personal reasons, I'm not sure I could face it.'

'For heaven's sake,' he exploded suddenly. 'This is the end of the twentieth century! You're more likely to have an accident on the way to the airport than when you're actually flying.'

She flinched at the scorn in his voice, and was about to tell him the very good reason why she had always avoided flying, but then she restrained herself. Wasn't it time she faced up to her fears and tried to conquer them? Just at that moment there was a knock on the door, which was then thrust open abruptly. John, her gardening neighbour, stood there, his burly frame nearly filling the doorway.

'Everything all right, Frances?' he enquired.

Frankie looked from the tall, roughly-dressed gardener to the elegant business man at the table, and was amused by the contrast.

'Everything's fine, John. As I told you, the gentleman is here on business, so there's nothing to worry about.'

John nodded, turned, and went away, closing the door behind him. Frankie turned back to Paul Hillwood to find him staring at the door.

'What was that about?' he demanded blankly.

'Don't worry.' Frankie laughed. 'John Seeley is my self-appointed watchdog. He was just checking up on you. If a stranger calls, he looks in after a time.'

'I'm glad you told him I was harmless,' her visitor commented with feeling. 'He looks pretty strong.'

'He is, but he is very kind to me. Incidentally, he is one of the assistants you referred to. If I do come to Istanbul, he'll look after this cottage for me and take care of any problems at the factory.'

'Will you come?'

She took a deep breath.

'Before I decide finally, tell me what I'd have to do exactly.'

He picked up some of the papers on the table.

'Here. There's an outline of the firm we are going to visit, and information as to what exactly we are trying to sell them. From you they will need details about the improvement in performance that your designs will provide, and details of some of the functions. Make sure you have facts and figures to back up what you say, and don't make any claims you're not sure about.'

She took the sheaf of papers he thrust at her, nervously aware of the commitment she was about to make. Paul Hillwood must have sensed her doubts, for he looked her straight in the eyes and spoke confidently.

'Don't worry about the flying. I'll be there to help you. And remember, you'll be going to Istanbul, one of the most exciting cities in the world. There will even be time to see some of the sights, I promise you.'

She tried to ignore her doubts, and smiled at him, chin lifted. She might not like him, but she felt she would be able to rely on him.

'Then I'll come with you.'

'Good,' he said, and turned back to the documents still on the table.

Frankie felt a sense of anti-climax. Once he had got her agreement he had instantly reverted to a cold, business-like person. Now he had found a folder containing the actual travel plans and was telling her what time he would meet her at the airport and that he would have her ticket with him. She began to feel like a child being given instructions about a school trip.

'Just give me the papers and I'll look at them later,' she said impatiently.

Reluctantly he did this, and then handed her a small white card.

'Here's my telephone number. Call me if you have any more questions.'

Briskly he replaced the remaining papers in his briefcase and stood ready to go. Once more he looked round the little room, so lacking in luxuries.

'I forgot to mention money,' he said thoughtfully. 'LRT will pay you a consultant's fee for the trip. I think you'll find it worth your while.'

Frankie was not particularly stung by the implied comment on her standard of decoration and furnishing, for she had always cheerfully acknowledged that this was not one of her strong points. However, she did feel a certain amount of malicious pleasure soon afterwards. When Paul Hillwood stepped out of the door he halted and looked up at the sky, where clouds were being whipped by the winds. He carried on up the path without looking down and tripped on an uneven flagstone! He ended on one knee, and although he stood upright immediately, unfortunate amounts of mud had been left behind on his beautiful tailoring.

'Oh, I'm sorry!' Frankie exclaimed. 'Let me get a cloth.'

'It doesn't matter,' he said through clenched teeth, wiping at the marks with his spotless handkerchief.

From the next garden John called urgently.

'Has your visitor hurt himself, Frances?'

'I thought everyone called you Frankie?' Paul Hillwood enquired, his attention momentarily distracted from his ruined suit.

'For some reason John prefers to call me Frances, though almost everybody else seems to think that Frankie suits me better.'

Once again he eyed the old jeans and sweatshirt.

'Yes, I can see,' he said without further comment, and made his way down the drive until he came to the car she had been working on.

'You should be able to afford a decent car after Istanbul,' he remarked.

He clearly meant this as an inducement, but Frankie was fuming as she followed him to the pavement where a sleek black car as spotless as his suit had been was parked. He shook hands briefly with her and got into the car.

'Make sure you leave plenty of time to get to the airport,' was his parting instruction.

As she gazed after him, John Seeley joined her.

'He looked smart enough till he got mud on his lovely suit,' he said. 'Who was he, anyway?'

'His name's Paul Hillwood, he likes facts, and he thinks my beautiful 1957 Aston Martin DB24 Mark III is a load of junk!' she said indignantly. 'Oh, and incidentally, I'm flying on a selling trip with him on Tuesday.'

John stood very still for a moment and then gave her a thoughtful glance.

'That should be interesting.'

2

Frankie went back into the cottage and took the tea tray into the kitchen where she began to wash the cups and saucers. Suddenly there was a crash as one of the saucers slipped from her suddenly heedless fingers and fell to the floor. She was going to Istanbul in less than two days' time!

Frankie's annual holidays in France were always preceded by long, ritual preparations, with lists carefully ticked and every detail double-checked. If such preparation was needed to cross the Channel, how could she fly thousands of miles at such short notice? Her first action was to abandon the washing-up and dash upstairs to find her passport.

With hasty fingers she opened the little red-backed document and checked the dates, then drew a sigh of relief. At least her passport was still valid! With that established, she sat down at the table and by the last of the daylight she went carefully through the papers that Paul Hillwood had given her. She had to admit that he was thorough, and fortunately he was also lucid. The travel itinerary was clearly laid out. As he had told her, they would fly from Manchester on Tuesday morning and she noted that she would have to be there by seven o'clock and would return to England on Friday. All that distance for three nights!

The rest of the day was spent on practical matters. She managed a little washing and ironing, and her meals became a peculiar assortment designed to use up the perishables in her refrigerator. After supper she retreated to the smaller of the cottage's two bedrooms. Its most prominent feature was a computer surrounded by up-to-the-minute equipment on a large desk which allowed Frankie to sit back occasionally and take relief from work in looking at the panoramic sweep of the

21

Yorkshire moors outside the window.

Apart from that, the room contained little but a swivel chair and filing cabinets. Here Frankie set to work systematically to master and organise all the material which she might be required to present to the firm in Istanbul. There was no panic. This was her world and she was happy in it. By midnight everything she needed was printed out and assembled in two files. Paul Hillwood would not be able to find fault with her when it came to work.

On Monday morning she arrived early at Pickard's modest premises in her twenty-four-year-old Mini, one of her earlier attempts at car restoration. One day, she had promised herself, she would arrive in all the glory of the Aston Martin, but for the present, her little car was reliable. As usual, John Seeley's old motorbike was already there before her, she noted. Frankie made her way to her own tiny office.

This morning, however, instead of

exchanging her warm coat for white overalls, she rapidly dialled an internal number on the telephone.

'Miss Beech?' she checked when her call was answered. 'This is Miss Green. I need to speak to Mr Pickard urgently. Can you tell me when he is free?'

She listened to the reply, and gave a short laugh.

'Oh, he was expecting me to call, was he? I'll come straight away then.'

She strode along the functional, uncarpeted corridors towards the office of Mr Frederick Pickard, founder, owner and manager of the firm, the man referred to so casually by Paul Hillwood as old Pickard. Well, he might be seventy-four, but he still ran the firm very efficiently.

In the outer office she was greeted by an elegant blonde in her fifties who rose at her entrance and gave her a cool smile.

'Mr Pickard is ready to see you, Miss Green,' Miss Beech said.

She opened the inner door and

ushered Frankie into the large, oak-panelled room where Frankie crossed the thick, velvet-pile carpet until she was facing the great polished, wood desk. Once Frederick Pickard had started to make money he had decided that as he spent more time at work than he did at home he might as well make sure that he had a setting he enjoyed. Now he sat in a large, leather chair, watching Frankie approach. Short but stout, virtually bald but for the white fringe of hair round his head, his face beamed as she neared him. He leaped up from his chair as she reached the desk, came from behind it to greet her, and embraced her.

'Give your granddad a kiss, then,' he instructed her.

She did as he bade her, while Miss Beech stood watching indulgently.

'Shall I make us some tea, Fred?' she enquired.

'Aye,' was the response, 'and make sure there are some of those shortcake biscuits, Diane.'

'No shortcakes for you in the morning, Fred,' he was told sternly. 'I'm watching your diet.'

With that, she left the room and grandfather and granddaughter settled themselves comfortably by the desk.

Frankie had been ten when her grandfather and Miss Beech had appeared unexpectedly to collect her from school and then break the news that her parents had been killed. From that day onwards, Fred Pickard had looked after her devotedly, turning to his secretary, Diane Beech, for any matters which he felt were beyond him. His wife had died young, and as most of his time was spent in his factory, that was where he took Frankie when she was not at school or with friends.

Although a man who would have loved sons to follow him, Frankie's mother had been his only child, and her death left only the young girl as a possible successor in the firm. He had therefore been delighted when workers told him how quickly Frankie seemed to pick up the intricacies of machines, understanding almost without explanation the theory behind the complicated processes. Quick to see how things were changing, Fred Pickard made sure his firm was not left behind when electronic engineering began to develop, and this proved to be very much to Frankie's taste.

Her mind loved the logic and order of the electronic processes, mentally tracing the pulses and patterns of power. When she had obtained her degree it was taken for granted that she would return to the firm, though Fred Pickard had advertised her present post and only appointed her when he was satisfied she was the best candidate, determined that it should not seem that she had got the job because of her family connections. Although the other workers knew of the relationship, outside his inner office door the behaviour of Mr Pickard and Miss Frances Green was carefully formal.

'I suppose you know what I've come

about,' Frankie observed. 'I had a visitor on Sunday from LRT. He said you knew he was coming. You might have warned me!'

Fred Pickard's smile grew broader.

'No point. LRT said he would explain everything, so I thought I'd let their man surprise you. What was he like?'

'Pompous,' she said bitterly. 'He was wearing a business suit, on a Sunday afternoon, and when he found me underneath the Aston Martin he tended to treat me like a half-witted garage mechanic!'

'Hurt your pride, did he? Well, you'll have to forgive him. LRT says he's one of their best men, so perhaps he knows how good he is. He was wearing the suit, incidentally, because he only got back from ten days in America that morning, so he probably wasn't in a very good mood.'

That would have explained the tiredness and tension, Frankie thought. Maybe she had been a little hard on him.

'I know that because he's already been on the phone to me this morning,' her grandfather added. 'I gather you've agreed to go to Istanbul with him tomorrow.'

At that moment, Diane Beech came in with a tray with tea things for three, and they waited while she poured the tea and then took a seat near the desk. Frankie noted that while she and Diane had shortcake biscuits, her grandfather was given one small, plain biscuit.

Diane Beech had been his secretary for twenty years. She knew everything about the firm and its business although, like Frankie, outside that closed office door it was always Mr Pickard and Miss Beech.

'Do you need any help, Frances?' she enquired.

She was one of the few people to address Frankie by her full name, declaring that it was a beautiful name for a girl, unlike the diminutive Frankie which she disliked intensely. Any attempts by over-friendly acquaintances

28

to shorten her own name to Di were met with frosty hostility.

'I probably need your help with packing,' the girl said gratefully. 'I'm not sure what I need for this type of trip or for Istanbul in November.'

'Don't worry. I'll be there this evening to pack for you. Now, what time have you got to be in Manchester?'

'Seven o'clock, so I'll have to leave just before six. I suppose I could park the Mini at the airport, but I'm hoping John Seeley will drive me there.'

'If he won't, I'll take you,' Diane Beech said decisively.

Frankie smiled gratefully, and then jumped as the telephone rang. Fred Pickard picked it up impatiently.

'Pickard here. Oh, Mr Hillwood. Yes, I have spoken to Miss Green.'

He listened, and a wicked grin spread across his face.

'Yes, I understand. Don't worry. I'll see that's all right.'

When he put down the telephone he was shaking with quiet laughter as he looked at the two enquiring faces.

'Your Mr Hillwood just wanted to make sure that you would be suitably dressed for a business trip. Apparently what you were wearing on Saturday didn't inspire him with confidence.'

She had not misjudged Mr Hillwood after all, Frankie decided indignantly, and looked at her two elders who were laughing unashamedly.

'I told him I didn't wear my best clothes under a car!' she raged.

Diane Beech put a comforting arm round her shoulders.

'Don't worry,' she said soothingly. 'I know you can look good.'

She had good cause to know. Twice a year, in spring and autumn, Diane Beech collected a reluctant Frankie and after ruthlessly purging her wardrobe of clothes which she considered out of date or past their best, took her on a shopping expedition for clothes for the coming season. Her taste in clothes was excellent, and it was thanks to her that Frankie found she always had the

30

appropriate clothes to wear for any occasion.

Now, with her usual efficiency and tact, Diane collected the tray and returned to her own office, leaving grandfather and granddaughter to deal with matters private to the two of them. Frankie looked across the desk at the plump, little figure.

'You know what the problem is with this trip, Granddad.'

He nodded sadly. The accident that had killed his beloved daughter and son-in-law had happened when a flight from Paris had crashed in a thunderstorm. Fred Pickard had steadfastly refused to fly ever since.

'How do you feel about it?' he asked.

Frankie shrugged indecisively.

'In some ways, the idea of flying terrifies me. But all my friends fly, usually several times a year, and if I never fly it means there are a lot of places I'll never be able to see. I've got to make the effort. There will always be the thought of my parents' death to

31

haunt me, but it's said that you are more likely to have an accident on the way to the airport than in the air.'

Her grandfather nodded slowly.

'You know my prayers will go with you,' he said softly.

Frankie went round to him and kissed him, and then went out to get on with her work. If he needed more comfort or reassurance, Diane Beech would see that he got it.

Frankie spent most of the rest of the day with John Seeley. When she had told Paul Hillwood that John was one of her assistants, she had been guiltily aware that she had been doing him less than justice. Nominally he was her second-in-command, but she knew that in many aspects of the work he was her equal. They had known each other since she first started school, when Frankie had been the cherished only child of doting parents, and John, three years older, was also an only child, but in very different circumstances, for his mother had died when he was a baby, leaving her child to the inadequate care of a father who neglected his son in favour of his friends at the pub.

Frankie had lost sight of John when she had gone on to an exclusive fee-paying school and had been surprised to find that he was the other applicant short-listed for the post she now held. She learned later that stubborn determination had enabled him to reach college and support his studies by part-time work, in spite of his father's scorn for his studious son. He seemed to pride himself on never showing emotion, and Frankie was surprised by his reaction when she told him where she was going.

'Istanbul? You're going to Istanbul?'

He looked positively excited.

'Just for a few nights. Would you be kind enough to drive me to the airport, John? It means leaving very early, but otherwise Miss Beech is willing to take me.'

'You know I'll take you,' he said immediately, and looked as if he was about to say more, but then he turned away.

It was nearing the end of a long, hard day when Diane Beech appeared and announced that she had come to take Frankie home to pack. Once they had left town, Frankie preceded the secretary along the narrow, winding roads, only looking back occasionally to see the small, highly-polished and bright red sports car that was following her. In cars, as in clothes, Diane's taste was for expensive simplicity.

Once in the cottage they had a snack meal before they began to tackle the packing, working together with the ease of affection as well as long familiarity. Ever since the death of her parents, Frankie had known that she could rely on Diane as much as on her grandfather. They came together. Each July, Fred Pickard would take his orphaned granddaughter for a fortnight's holiday to a villa in Normandy, and each time Diane Beech would accompany them.

Fred said that a young girl needed a

woman around the place, even when Frankie had turned twenty, and she suspected that he took Diane along automatically now, unwilling to spend time apart from the woman who shared most of his life. Diane had eased life for Frankie, however. She was the one who had persuaded Fred Pickard that his granddaughter did indeed need a place of her own after she left university, and no longer needed to remain under his watchful eye in his house. He had agreed grudgingly only when he found that John Seeley would be her neighbour.

'He'll keep an eye on her,' he had told Diane.

Once the packing was completed the two women sat chatting.

'Granddad's going to be anxious tomorrow,' Frankie ventured.

'You mean while you're flying? I know. I'll have to find some little problem at work, something that will distract him and get him annoyed about the time you are due to take off. Then perhaps he'll forget about you for a while.'

'I'll be thinking of him, and of you.'

'I'm sure you will. Call as soon as possible to let us know you are safe.'

Diane left soon afterwards, instructing Frankie to get a good night's sleep. The girl doubted if this would be possible, but in fact she fell asleep quickly, and the alarm woke her to darkness and the sound of Yorkshire rain drumming on the roof. At first she lay there drowsily, wondering why she had to get up so early, and then memory flooded back and she sat up abruptly. She was starting the day in Yorkshire, but she would end it under the skies of Istanbul!

Frankie showered and dressed quickly in the dark trouser suit and white silk shirt that Diane had recommended, and then had a cup of coffee, all she felt she could swallow that morning. Promptly at half-past five, there was a knock at the door, and John Seeley stood ready to take her luggage to the Mini, just visible in the growing light. Frankie switched off the house lights and locked the front door. As she got to the car, John Seeley offered her a little book.

'I thought you might like this,' he said a little gruffly.

A quick look showed her that it was a guide to Istanbul. He waved her thanks aside.

'I'll drive, shall I? You've got too much to think about to concentrate on the road.'

He started the car and they set off, while Frankie wondered where and why he had got the guide. She looked at his calm, impassive profile. In spite of the fact that they were neighbours, John was a very private person.

'Have you got your passport?' he demanded abruptly.

Frankie patted her pocket and nodded.

'How do you feel now?' he asked her.

Frankie gave a hollow laugh.

'I now understand exactly what

37

people mean when they say they've got butterflies in their tummy,' she announced, and got an unsympathetic grin in return.

The drive went smoothly and they joined the motorway. Frankie felt herself growing calmer, until John stamped on the brake with a muttered exclamation. Tail lights glowed red ahead as far as the eye could see.

'There must be a hold-up, possibly an accident,' he snapped. 'Fortunately we've got time to spare.'

But progress was painfully slow, and sometimes they were stationary for several minutes at a time. The spare time was gradually eroded, and Frankie had to stop herself looking at her watch every few seconds. Then, finally, they passed the obstruction, a lorry which had shed its load, and John stepped on the accelerator, nudging the speed limit whenever he could.

The signs to the airport were growing more frequent, then it was the next turn-off. They swept along the slip road and between the maze of hotels, carparks and airport buildings, screeching to a halt under a concrete roof. John had the door open instantly and handed Frankie the shoulder bag that would be Frankie's hand luggage. He himself carried her suitcase. They burst through the glass doors into the check-in area.

The first person Frankie saw was Paul Hillwood, pacing impatiently up and down. Glancing at the clock, she saw that it was exactly seven o'clock!

3

Frankie took three seconds to pause and compose herself, and then advanced smiling towards the tall figure.

'Good morning, Mr Hillwood!' she said sweetly. 'I'm glad we are both on time.'

He spun round and looked twice before he recognised her. His eyes narrowed suddenly as he assessed her appearance, so different from that of their previous meeting.

'Am I suitably dressed?' she challenged, and he had the grace to colour.

'Very suitably dressed, Miss Green.'

His gaze shifted to John, waiting patiently with the suitcase.

'You've met John Seeley, my neighbour,' Frankie reminded him. 'He was kind enough to drive me here this morning.'

'Oh, yes, the watchdog,' Paul Hillwood said coldly.

There was a moment while the two men regarding each other warily. Paul Hillwood broke the silence.

'I'm sure Miss Green is very grateful for your help.'

He sounded condescending, as though thanking a servant. The two men nodded stiffly at each other. Frankie was aware of the instinctive antagonism between them. Frankie speculated that Paul might resent the fact that John had witnessed his undignified fall on Sunday, but what was it about Paul which had roused such instant dislike in the normally placid John?

'It's time to check in,' Paul Hillwood announced, leading the way to one of the desks that lined the wall.

There Frankie handed him her passport, and he dealt with the booking clerk. As he was tucking tickets and passports into his inside pocket, John stepped forward and placed Frankie's suitcase on the conveyor belt that whirled it away.

'The flight is delayed for a short while, so we've got about ninety minutes before it leaves. Would you like a coffee?' Paul Hillwood asked.

The invitation was pointedly directed at Frankie, who looked uncertainly at John, but he smiled comfortably at her, obviously unmoved by the snub.

'I must go, Frances. You know I like to be at work early so that I can have everything ready for the day. Enjoy the trip and don't worry about work. I'll take care of any problems.'

Then he turned on his heel and walked briskly to the exit, ignoring the other man. Frankie suddenly felt lonely and abandoned and looked uncertainly at Paul Hillwood, wondering what they should do next, but he showed no hesitation.

'We'll go through to the departure lounge now,' he announced, leading the way through gateways and past officials to whom he displayed the relevant documents.

In the departure lounge, Frankie felt

overwhelmed by the acres of carpet and bright shop displays. Then, through great glass windows, she saw the aeroplanes themselves, sleek monsters bearing the insignia of the many different airlines and countries. She felt a shiver of apprehension.

Paul Hillwood followed her gaze.

'We'll have that coffee now,' he said firmly.

Some time later, clutching her empty coffee cup and nodding dutifully at intervals, Frankie decided that her original estimation of him had been correct. He was one of the most boring men in the world! All he could talk about was machine tools and the sales policy of his company. Five more minutes and she would scream. But just before that point was reached he looked at his watch, stopped in mid-sentence, and smiled at her smugly.

'Well, Miss Green, have I bored you?'

Too polite to reply with the truth, she simply looked at him.

'Good,' he commented. 'That was

what I was trying to do. It was one way to stop you worrying about your first flight.'

He grinned at her half-grateful, half-exasperated reaction and rose gracefully to his feet.

'It's time to board the plane now, however.'

In a short time, she emerged from a tunnel to find herself in the doorway of their plane, and was ushered to a window seat by a smart stewardess. By the time she had fastened her seat-belt, seen how all the luggage was safely stowed away and looked curiously round the cabin, the aeroplane roared to life and moved away. Impressed by the skill with which the pilot manoeuvred the great machine smoothly over the ground, she was aware of it pausing for a while, and then suddenly it thrust forward fast, and then faster. Soon it would be taking off.

Her suppressed fears returned and she grew tense. Unexpectedly she felt a warm hand cover her icy-cold fist.

'Relax,' Paul Hillwood said soothingly. 'Close your eyes if you like.'

She did as he suggested, and heard how the rumble of the wheels on concrete suddenly ended, and there was a peculiar, weightless feeling for a second.

'We are in the air now,' her companion murmured.

She opened her eyes. Outside the window swirling white mist surrounded the plane. Then, abruptly, they were above the clouds and the morning sun shone brilliantly down from a blue sky on to the buoyant white clouds. Frankie gasped.

'This is a moment I always enjoy,' Paul Hillwood told her. 'You take off in wet, cold weather, and moments later there's nothing but sunshine.'

Frankie smiled at him tremulously.

'It's magical,' she said in awe.

She did not tell him how the ghosts of her parents had haunted her during those first few minutes. Now they had faded, their tragedy in the past and their daughter left to the present. As the aeroplane flew steadily onwards she settled in her seat and explored the in-flight magazine, enjoyed the experience of breakfast on a tray, and rejected the offer of cut-price perfumes. Time passed, and she became aware that Paul Hillwood was looking at her with mild amusement.

'Your fear of flying seems to be fading rapidly.'

'I feel all right now but I'm not looking forward to the landing.'

He shrugged.

'I've experienced it hundreds of times now, so it has become a matter of routine for me. It's refreshing to watch your reactions, though.'

This sounded a little patronising, she thought, then remembered how he had held her hand, and decided to overlook it.

'But you're going all over the world, to all the great cities. Isn't that exciting?' she said.

'I suppose it was at first, but now I've

spent nearly ten years in sales for LRT, and really, all I see are airports, identical international hotels and identical office blocks. There are still a few places I find exciting, New York, for example.'

'And Istanbul?'

He nodded firmly.

'Most definitely Istanbul. But I'm afraid I'm getting tired of the constant travelling on behalf of other people. I'd like to have my own firm, make my own decisions. But that takes money.'

She looked at him, wondering about the man behind the cool, business-like exterior, and tried to extract some information tactfully.

'Did you come to the airport by yourself this morning, or did someone bring you?'

His lips twitched.

'No, Miss Green, I am not married.'

So much for tact! Frankie relapsed into silence, occasionally peering out of the window, where thinning cloud allowed glimpses of a patchwork of fields and towns far below. It was after the ever-attentive stewardesses had offered them mid-flight coffee that Paul Hillwood restarted the conversation.

'I understand that your Mr Pickard has been running the firm for a very long time.'

'He started the firm immediately he came out of the army after the war,' she told him.

'So he must be well over seventy now. Have you ever wondered what will happen to the firm when he stops running it?'

She nodded, frowning. The fact that her grandfather could not go on for ever had been brought home to her several times recently, and she had heard other members of the staff speculating on what would happen after him. He had always run the firm by himself, controlling every aspect of the business and he had done it well, but it meant that now there was no obvious successor ready to take over. She knew the task was beyond her, even if she had wanted it. Her interests lay in the actual application of electronics, not in management.

Paul Hillwood studied her expression.

'I know you jumped down my throat when you thought I was trying to poach you from Pickard's,' he said cautiously, 'but all the same, there's no need for you to worry. An electronic engineer with your abilities will always be able to get a job. As you told me, you have had other approaches.'

But it wouldn't be like Pickard's, she thought. Where else would she be given the same freedom to develop her ideas? In a large firm she would have to be a team player, fit into the corporate jigsaw, instead of setting her own goals.

'I'm sorry,' her companion said awkwardly, 'I didn't mean to upset you. It's just that facts are facts.'

Silence fell again, and this time it lasted until the announcement that they would soon be starting to descend to Istanbul. Soon Frankie was conscious of the plane gradually swooping lower, of the land rising to meet them, and she felt her tension return. Then, once again, a firm hand gripped hers. As she found the slow descent even harder to face than the take-off, her own grip tightened in return. Suddenly there was a bump, and the sound of the wheels in contact with the ground again, and gradually the headlong speed grew less and they eventually came to a halt. Frankie realised that she had been holding her breath, and gasped deeply, releasing Paul Hillwood's hand. He shook it ruefully, and she perceived how her grip had marked his hand. As he flexed his fingers she saw the red marks of her nails.

'Remind me to wear thick gloves for the return journey,' he commented.

For the first time Frankie experienced the mingled suspense and boredom of waiting to collect her luggage from the carousel. With both suitcases safely recovered, the two of them walked past the customs officers and saw, just beyond, a dark-eyed young man in a chauffeur's uniform, holding a piece of cardboard hand-lettered with 'Hillwood, Green'. Paul took Frankie by the elbow, steered her towards the man and identified himself. The chauffeur greeted them with a brilliant smile, though he looked at Frankie with surprise as well as admiration before leading them out to where a black limousine stood waiting.

'I work for the Yilmaz brothers and I am to take you to the hotel,' he said eagerly. 'Then, if you want transport while you are in Istanbul, I shall be happy to drive you wherever you wish to go.'

The car drew away from the airport and Paul Hillwood settled back, though Frankie was peering eagerly out of the window, but the car drove too fast for her to gain any real impression of the city and its outskirts before they drew up outside an imposing hotel.

'This hotel is Swiss-run and very

comfortable indeed,' Paul Hillwood murmured.

While the chauffeur carried in the luggage, Paul led Frankie confidently through the entrance hall to the reception desk, where a beautiful, dark-eyed girl greeted them with courteous warmth. However, like the chauffeur, she looked at Frankie with some surprise before leaning forward confidentially and explaining something to Paul with apologetic shrugs. He lifted his eyebrows, but did not appear particularly upset when he turned to Frankie.

'I'm afraid the firm and therefore the hotel have made the same mistake as I did,' he said with wry amusement. 'It was assumed that you were a man, and one suite has been booked for the two of us. However,' he added hastily as Frankie opened her mouth to protest, 'there are two bedrooms, so we can share it in perfect respectability. Otherwise we can have two single rooms, but personally I would prefer the suite.'

He was the seasoned traveller who knew best. Frankie bowed to his wishes, and they and their luggage were soon entering the sitting-room of a suite on the top floor of the hotel. Frankie stepped through the door, gasped, and stood stock-still in amazement. It was a corner room and the two walls forming the corner were virtually all floor-to-ceiling glass. From this lofty position, the vast panoramic vista of Istanbul and its waterways was laid out before them. Mosques raised their domes among the crowded buildings and sunlight glittered on the sea. Frankie remembered the grey, windswept view from her own window that morning and stood with her face close to the glass, drinking in the scene.

'Isn't it beautiful?' she said in awe.

'Very striking,' Paul Hillwood said, sparing the view one quick glance and then touring the suite. 'Now, I suggest I take this room to the right, and you take the other. Please note that I am letting you have the full bathroom, while I only have a shower.'

Obediently Frankie took her luggage into the room indicated and carefully unpacked and hung up her clothes. It did not take long, and she emerged to find Paul Hillwood on the telephone and coffee and sandwiches being delivered by room service.

'No time for a proper lunch,' he said, indicating the food.

Frankie helped herself and stood gazing out of the window until he had finished his call and came to stand by her.

'The delay at Manchester this morning is causing a slight problem,' he stated. 'I will call on the Yilmaz Brothers this afternoon, but it's only a courtesy call, so you needn't come. Then I've arranged to call at our Embassy, to check up on a few regulations. I'll probably be back about six o'clock.'

'What do I do?' Frankie demanded.

He looked at her vaguely, his mind clearly already occupied with the coming interviews. For the moment she was irrelevant.

'Stay here,' he said. 'Read, watch television, have a rest. I suppose you could wander out a little, get the feel of Istanbul, so long as you're here when I get back. Now, if you'll excuse me, I'll go and freshen up.'

He vanished into his room to reappear ten minutes later complete with briefcase. He muttered a farewell, and left purposefully. Frankie told herself that there was no reason to feel abandoned and that she needed time to recover from the events of the day anyway. She sank down on a deep couch and picked up the telephone, but when she got through to Pickard's she was told that both Mr Pickard and Miss Beech were in a meeting, so she simply left a message telling them she had arrived safely.

An hour later she had read Paul Hillwood's discarded paper, flicked through the television channels and got bored with the English-language news and films, and was feeling decidedly restless. She looked rebelliously through the window at the waiting city. Why should she wait here like a good little girl for Mr Hillwood to return? Swiftly she changed into a sheath dress covered by a light jacket that seemed appropriate for the October sunshine of Istanbul and took the lift to the ground floor, then marched through the main doors, only to stop abruptly on the steps of the hotel.

This was the first time she had been by herself in a strange city, one completely different to anything she had known before. Suddenly she was homesick for the grey skies of Yorkshire and the reassuring presence of John Seeley next door. The doorman approached her, a very tall man sporting a very impressive curved moustache.

'Can I help you, madam? Do you need directions to anywhere?'

She smiled shyly and shook her head, but she could not simply stand there while he watched her, so she took her first steps away from the hotel and into this strange new world. An hour later she found her way back, feeling mentally battered. She had been unprepared for the impact of a city which seethed with life and vigour and where figures from the Arabian Nights sauntered along beside others who would not have been out of place anywhere in the UK. Occasionally she saw a sign in English or even heard a few words of her own language, but for the rest of the time she was buffeted by the sound of strange tongues. Street traders spoke to her, holding out their wares, but she could only smile and shrug her shoulders.

4

Once back at the hotel she was reluctant to return to the isolation of the suite. If she sat in the reception area she would see Paul Hillwood arrive and could intercept him, so she gratefully leaned back in a comfortable chair and watched the busy passage of people in the lobby.

It was already six o'clock, she realised, and the bar was growing busy. She could hear the buzz of conversation and the chink of ice in glasses so she signalled to one of the waiters and was soon sipping her own drink contentedly. The half-empty glass was standing on the table by the side of her chair as she looked to see if Paul Hillwood was among a group who had just come in, and she jumped slightly when there was a slight cough by her side. She looked up in surprise at a stocky, middle-aged man whose expensive suit did its best to disguise his girth. The man had a pleasantly ugly face, and was smiling down at her.

'May I sit here?' he asked, indicating the empty chair by her side.

A swift looked informed Frankie that there were many other seats available. She might be alone in a strange city, but Fred Pickard's granddaughter was not about to allow herself to be picked up by a stranger. Instead of a reply the man received a steely, inhospitable glare, but his smile only grew wider.

'You must excuse my approaching you,' he said in a strong European accent. 'I believe you are here with my friend, Paul Hillwood, and I was hoping to meet him.'

Another salesman? Well, at least he knew Paul. Her expression became less forbidding.

'I'm waiting for him now,' she admitted.

'Then perhaps I can join you and we can wait together. Please, let me buy you another drink.'

He took the chair beside her and introduced himself as Dr Schmidt. He seemed to be an expert at small talk. He was obviously a business man, and seemed inquisitive about Paul Hillwood's mission to Istanbul, and her own part in it. She supposed it was natural curiosity, but her native Yorkshire caution made her reluctant to tell him too much, especially when his questions became rather too specific and probing, and it was with some relief that she finally spotted Paul Hillwood coming slowly through the door.

'Paul!' she called, standing up and waving to attract his attention.

She saw him recognise her and begin to wave, and then he saw her companion. His face grew cold and set, and he strode towards the two of them with scant regard for the people in his way, until he stood confronting the other man.

'Schmidt!'

The middle-aged man, completely

relaxed where he sat, looked up at him with a sly smile.

'Mr Paul Hillwood! How nice to see you again, especially after the pleasant chat I have had with your companion. Will you join us for a drink?'

Paul Hillwood looked down at him without speaking. Dr Schmidt sighed mockingly.

'Obviously you prefer not to. What a pity!'

Dr Schmidt turned to Frankie.

'Unfortunately it looks as if I must go now, but I hope to speak to you again.'

He stood up with no appearance of haste, bent his head in farewell to Frankie, smiled at Paul Hillwood, and sauntered away. Paul Hillwood seized Frankie's arm in a tight grip.

'What have you told him?'

'About what?' she queried. 'Stop hurting my arm!'

His grip slackened but his tone was still urgent.

'About why we are in Istanbul!'

'Nothing!' she protested.

'Are you sure?'

'Of course! What is the matter with you? I thought he seemed a bit too curious, so I was careful to tell him as little as possible.'

Paul's hand fell from her arm, and she rubbed it gingerly.

'He said he was your friend, but obviously that isn't true. Who is he?'

'He's a spy!'

Her eyes widened in horror and she was silent as they returned to their suite, where Paul questioned Frankie carefully, finally conceding that she appeared to have been safely discreet.

'If I'd known you would start talking to the first stranger to approach you, I'd have told you to stay in the room!'

Her eyes were dancing with anger.

'And do you think I would have obeyed? I've told you that I was perfectly safe in the reception area and that I didn't tell him anything about why we are here!'

Frankie was annoyed by his interrogation, but uneasily aware of her own ignorance about the characters who peopled this strategically-sited city. Reluctant to invite more reproach for talking to a stranger, she did not ask for more information about the mysterious Dr Schmidt.

Finally they sat in silence, oblivious of the city lights blazing invitingly below them, suddenly both conscious that it had been a long, hard day.

'I was going to take you out for dinner and show you Istanbul by night,' Paul said wearily. 'Unfortunately I don't think I've got the energy even to face the hotel restaurant. Do you mind if I have something sent up?'

They dined on salad, cold meats and cheese, followed by little pastries sticky with syrup, and it was soon after nine when they agreed that it was time for bed. Frankie hesitated at her bedroom door.

'How do you say good-night to a man when you're sharing his suite but not his room?' she enquired.

Paul gave her a brief smile.

'I've no idea, Miss Frankie Green. I've never been in this situation before either. So, good-night!'

'Good-night.'

On her first night in the exotic city of Istanbul, Frankie was fast asleep well before ten o'clock.

By eight o'clock the following morning, Paul Hillwood was watching in fascinated horror as she did her best to sample all the varied delights of the breakfast buffet while he restricted himself to orange juice and cereal.

'I'm hungry,' she told him. 'I didn't have a proper meal at all yesterday, and I don't know what's going to happen today.'

'Well, at least you won't starve,' he commented as she worked her way through her piled plate.

'Remember, I'm from Yorkshire. We like a good breakfast before a hard day's work.'

By nine o'clock, the chauffeur from Yilmaz Brothers had called for them. Frankie wore a dark grey tailored skirt and jacket over a cream blouse. Her blonde hair was gathered into a neat coil at the nape of her neck. Her blue eyes were discreetly shadowed, and as far as appearance went, she was the perfect business woman. Inwardly, however, she could not help being nervous. She had never been in direct contact with customers before, let alone partly responsible for trying to pin down a large sale. She glanced sideways at Paul Hillwood, immaculate in his dark business suit and white shirt with a sober tie, grateful that she had him to rely on and guide her.

The light, airy, functional Yilmaz offices could have been in any big city. The only surprise was that there were three brothers when somehow Frankie had only expected two. They were alert, friendly, intelligent and business-like, carefully checking the specifications and capabilities of everything they were considering. Paul had obviously informed them the previous afternoon that the electronics engineer accompanying him was a woman, and if they felt this was unusual they were too polite to show it.

Before lunch, her personal contribution was negligible, and she sat quietly by, free to appreciate Paul's knowledge and skill as a salesman. He was the master of his subject, patient and thorough, so that any potential customer would have felt totally reassured that they could rely on what he said. Finally they broke for lunch. Frankie welcomed the break, aware that soon she would have to play her part. Paul Hillwood drew her apart unobtrusively.

'Any worries?'

She shook her head.

'I don't think so. I know what I'm talking about, and they are so nice that I don't feel half as nervous as I did.'

He gave his occasional fleeting smile and some of the tension went out of her poise. At least he would not have to worry about her!

In the afternoon they did indeed move on to her area of expertise, and the three brothers were obviously impressed by her quiet confidence. The only bad moment came when one of the brothers wanted confirmation that a certain device could be relied on to perform a particular minute part of a complicated task. Frankie hesitated. The design was hers and had not yet progressed beyond the prototype, though she had assured Pickard's, who in turn had assured LRT, that it would work. Now the brothers were waiting for her answer, and she remembered what Paul had told her on the Saturday and settled for complete honesty.

'I can't give you one hundred per cent guarantee,' she told them frankly, 'because this hasn't yet been tested in working conditions for any length of time. What I can say is that I designed it and have checked every detail, and that I am as sure as it is possible to be that it will perform well.'

This seemed to satisfy the brothers, and she saw Paul nodding approvingly.

By four o'clock the meeting was

closed for the day, with warm hand-shakes all round. The car and chauffeur were waiting in the street.

'Back to the hotel?' the chauffeur asked, but Paul hesitated and turned to Frankie.

'Why don't I take you to see some of the main sights?' he asked her. 'That's if you're not too tired. There are still a couple of hours before we need to get back and think about dinner.'

She sat upright eagerly.

'Please, you must show me some-thing of Istanbul. I can't go back home and say I've only seen some offices and the hotel.'

Paul dismissed the chauffeur and decided the obvious place to start was the famed Topkapi Palace, and Frankie was amazed at the range and beauty of the buildings and their contents. It was the Treasury which awed her, however, with its overwhelming collection of riches.

'It's all too much,' she exclaimed. 'Can you imagine anyone having so much wealth? Would you like it?'

Paul Hillwood nodded slowly.

'Never underrate the power of money. I've met some very rich men during the past few years and I've seen the power they have. But I can't imagine I'll ever be like them,' he told her.

She remembered what he had said about wanting to start his own firm if he only had the money.

She continued to be dazzled by the mixture of Asian and European, old and new, Christian and Moslem, as they toured the city until at last they both confessed themselves exhausted and sought refuge in a small coffee house. It was getting dark, and the homebound traffic was growing heavy.

'Getting back to the hotel is simple,' Paul assured Frankie. 'All we've got to do is go down to the coast road and take a taxi.'

It should have been easy, but the coast road proved to be a non-stop river of several lanes of traffic as thousands of Turks headed for home. They hesitated on the pavement for some time, wondering how long they would have to wait before the traffic would ease off. When it became clear that that might take several hours, Paul acted decisively.

'Trust me,' he said as he seized her hand, and strode out into the traffic.

Drawn irresistibly along by his firm grip, she closed her eyes, and could not believe it when she opened them to find herself safe on the other side.

'How did you know we could do that safely?' she asked in amazement.

'I didn't,' Paul admitted. 'I just didn't want to spend the rest of the evening on that pavement!'

Now they were on the right side of the road they found a taxi fairly easily, only to find that progress became painfully slow as every driver fought for an advantage. Eventually the hotel was reached, and that night they dined in its restaurant. Looking round unobtrusively, Frankie was glad to see no sign of the mysterious Dr Schmidt. Afterwards Paul was busy with his lap-top computer, while Frankie curled up on the couch and divided her attention between the television and idly watching her companion. Finally he closed the computer and looked across at her.

'What did you think of your day?'

'I enjoyed all of it,' she told him. 'I like people who know what they are doing, and that applied to both you and the Yilmaz brothers.'

'Let me return the compliment. You were quite impressive yourself,' he told her, to her great pleasure.

She knew him well enough now to be sure that he was sincere.

'This afternoon's taste of sight-seeing was marvellous as well, but I was glad you were with me. I would have been completely lost on my own.'

He went to the window and looked out.

'It's a great place is Istanbul.'

'Which used to be called Constantinople, for some reason.'

'Which used to be called Stumbul, Kushta, Gosdantnubolic, Tsarigrad and quite a few other names, but now it's Istanbul. It just shows what a long and cosmopolitan history it has had.'

'My grandfather will love hearing about it,' Frankie said without thinking.

Paul turned to her.

'Your grandfather?'

'My mother's father,' she said hastily. 'He's an old man now and doesn't do much travelling.'

Mentally she apologised to Fred Pickard for making him sound so ancient and feeble.

'What about your parents? Won't they be interested as well?'

'They are both dead,' she said quietly. 'In fact they were killed in a plane crash when I was young. That's the reason why I've never flown before.'

She looked up when he did not respond and saw that he was looking at her with horror.

'And I treated you like a timid little

idiot!' he apologised. 'You must have hated me.'

She summoned up a grin.

'You weren't to know, and, yes, I didn't like you very much at first, but I'm glad I've come with you now. I won't be afraid to fly again, and I am seeing Istanbul.'

His smile was rueful.

'I wasn't too keen on you when you climbed out from under that old wreck of a car. Still, you've cleaned up quite well.'

Shared laughter brought them still closer together, and now Frankie ventured some enquiries.

'You said you weren't married. Does that mean you haven't anyone you're close to?'

He shook his head.

'There have been one or two women whom I would have liked the opportunity to know better, but you can't develop a relationship when you're never in the same place for more than a few days. Women get tired of dates broken at the last minute and duty-free perfume instead of an evening together. I always seem to end up sending them presents when they marry someone else.'

They sat together on the couch.

'Things may improve, however. In the last year I have spent time organising and managing the sales force as well as travelling. Perhaps one day I'll get a job based in England and send other people out to the ends of the earth to sell things for LRT.'

'Talking about selling,' she interrupted, 'what's going to happen tomorrow? Will you want me with you?'

Immediately, he was once again the efficient businessman.

'I want you to come with me in the morning, just in case they have thought of any more questions for you. But if we have made the sale, and I think we have, then I can deal with the afternoon's affairs.'

'If I'm not wanted then, can I go off and explore a little more by myself?'

'I don't see why not. We can get a plan of the city from the hotel. Incidentally, I'd better give you some Turkish money.'

From his briefcase he produced handfuls of notes of such high denominations that she protested, but he waved her objections aside.

'It looks a lot, but in fact all you have to do is ignore the last three noughts. Anyway, most places will probably take English money.'

She tucked the notes into her handbag.

'Thank you very much,' she said, then hesitated. 'I can't go on calling you Mr Hillwood any longer. It sounds far too formal.'

'I think,' he said, 'that as we are not only travelling and working together but also sharing accommodation that you may now call me Paul. That just leaves the problem of what I call you. Would you like to be Frances or Frankie?'

She frowned.

'It's difficult to decide,' she pondered. 'As I told you, usually people call me Frankie. My grandfather calls me Frankie because he wanted me to be a boy. I was Frances at school, but at work people call me Frankie because I deal mostly with men and it seems to help everyone to ignore the gender difference. In other words, take your choice.'

'I'll think about it,' he informed her, and suddenly gave a great yawn, apologising. 'I'm sorry, but I'm ready for a shower and bed.'

She scrambled to her feet.

'Me, too.'

That night, they parted more like old friends.

5

'Do you want to check again?' Paul enquired innocently. 'I think there may be one or two meats that you haven't tried yet.'

Frankie smiled at him cheerfully, quite at her ease for this second breakfast.

'You may be accustomed to hotels offering you all these goodies, but I have to make my own toast and coffee each morning,' she pointed out.

She felt light-hearted. The trip to Istanbul was turning out very well. She was confident that she had performed her part in the business negotiations satisfactorily, and Paul Hillwood had proved a much more pleasant companion than she had expected. Now all she had to do was stand ready to field any further queries this morning, and then she would be free to explore some more of the sights of Istanbul.

'I see you're wearing yet another outfit,' Paul observed.

Frankie looked down at her navy-blue outfit.

'The technical name is a coat-dress,' she informed him loftily. 'Miss Beech chose it for me. She is an expert at that. In fact she is at most things she does.'

Paul sipped his coffee thoughtfully before he spoke again.

'She sounded a most impressive woman on the telephone. Tell me, what do you think she would do if she didn't work at Pickard's?'

Taken by surprise, Frankie laughed at the idea.

'What a peculiar question! I can't imagine her doing anything else. It's her life. She's been there ever since I can remember.'

'I see,' Paul said a little heavily, and didn't speak again until he pointed out that it would soon be time to leave.

The morning passed much as Paul had predicted. She only had to deal

78

with a couple of minor points, and from the number of questions on delivery time and price negotiations it seemed clear that the brothers might well be ready to conclude the deal. With their agreement, she stayed for lunch, then took her leave with much hand-shaking, and found herself free to explore wherever she wanted.

'Enjoy yourself,' had been Paul's parting instruction. 'I think I'll have good news for you this evening.'

The car with the friendly chauffeur was at her disposal, but after he had taken her to an open space which was apparently called the Hippodrome she sent him away as the map provided by the hotel indicated that most places she wanted to visit were now within walking distance. She had remembered to bring John Seeley's guide book, and it told her that she was actually on the site of chariot races and massacres in previous centuries.

Two hours later, Frankie's head was whirling with impressions of delicate minarets, great domes and stately buildings, green gardens and the ruins of towering walls. Above all she was aware of the people — lively, exuberant, regarding her with the same friendly interest as she felt in them, even though an awful lot of them kept offering to sell her carpets!

Frankie decided to make for something which sounded comparatively peaceful in contrast. At breakfast she heard someone mention Yerebatan Cistern, only to have his companion tell him that she wasn't going to waste her time looking at a water-tank! However, if the tourists authorities thought it worth showing on their map it must have some interest.

The Cistern was not hard to find, though the small building above ground did not promise much. Once Frankie had entered and gone down a flight of steps, though, she found herself in a magical world. Dark waters lapped the walkways that criss-crossed the vast subterranean chamber, its roof supported by hundreds of pillars. A golden glow of light increased to show the distant aisles and then faded away, while the quiet murmur of music increased the theatre of the spectacle.

Frankie was absorbed by both the visual appeal and the function of this man-made underground lake, until she chanced to look up. Across the water that divided the walkways she found herself staring at Dr Schmidt. Hastily she turned away and made for a far corner, trusting that he had not seen her, but when she looked back she found that he was much closer, his eyes fixed on her. Then followed almost five minutes of hide-and-seek as Frankie tried to evade him in the maze of walkways, but there was only one exit from the Yerebatan Cistern, and she would have to emerge into an open, brightly-lit area to reach the steps to the surface.

Her heart was beating furiously as she reproached herself for her careless attitude. How could she forget that Turkey, unlike her own island home, was bordered by countries noted for their ruthlessness? Thinking about what Paul had said, she was aware that some aspects of her work could well be adapted to weaponry. Perhaps Schmidt's employers saw her as a useful prize, a promising electronic engineer whose youth and femininity would make her easy to intimidate.

Fighting down the rising panic, she set herself to mislead and elude her pursuer. At one moment she thought she had succeeded, but then she was suddenly bathed in the betraying golden glow, exposed to Schmidt's view before she hurried out of the light. Finally she saw her opportunity and dashed for the stairs, climbing them two at a time. Above ground, in the open air with people around her, it would be more difficult to ambush her.

This might be true, but she soon saw Schmidt appear at the exit to the Cistern as she hurried across the square. What could she do next? At this moment someone spoke to her. Distracted, she swung round. A thin, little man in a brown suit which had obviously been passed on by someone bigger was smiling at her a little forlornly.

'What did you say?' she demanded, her eyes still on Schmidt as he stood looking round, obviously trying to locate her.

'Would you like to come and see my cousin's carpet shop? There are many beautiful carpets, and his prices are very reasonable.'

The little man was scarcely a forceful representative and was turning away even before she replied, his dejected attitude showing that he was accustomed to refusals. She grabbed him by the arm.

'Of course I want to see carpets,' she said with great firmness. 'Take me there now. Quickly!'

The man scurried along by her side in grateful amazement, scarcely able to keep up with her determined stride. Surely no spy would dare try to kidnap her when she was viewing carpets, she thought.

An hour later, she emerged from the carpet shop with two small silk rugs lovingly wrapped up under her arm, and at her request, the happy shopkeeper beckoned a taxi that was cruising by. It was not yet rush-hour and the traffic was comparatively light. Frankie was looking forward to reaching the hotel reasonably quickly when the driver braked suddenly. The door opened, and Dr Schmidt climbed into the vehicle and sat down as the taxi sped away. Frankie sat bolt upright, staring at him in disbelief.

'Good afternoon, Miss Green,' was the doctor's greeting. 'How fortunate that we can share a taxi!'

'Are you kidnapping me?' she demanded bluntly.

'Good gracious, no!' he protested with glib sincerity. 'I assure you that the taxi will deliver us both safely at the hotel in time. However, he is going to take a roundabout route, I'm afraid.'

Frankie slipped off one shoe and then hefted it in her hand.

'If you try to touch me I'll hit you with this,' she warned him crisply.

He moved a little farther away.

'Please, Miss Green! I assure you that all I want to do is have a little talk, which could be to our mutual advantage.'

'What about?' she asked cautiously.

'Business, what else? I understand that you and Mr Hillwood are here to negotiate with a well-known Turkish firm. As a fellow businessman I am naturally interested in what you are trying to sell to them. In fact, Miss Green, I made some telephone calls after our first meeting and I found that you already have quite a reputation as an electronic engineer. Some details about your work would be particularly fascinating and, as I said, you might find it rewarding to talk to me. I am sure that Mr Hillwood is equally interested in everything you can tell him, but I am prepared to match whatever he is offering you.'

His tone was pleasant, with no hint of a threat, but the fact remained that he was keeping her in the taxi against her will. At this moment the taxi driver, who had shown no sign of interest in what was happening between his passengers, braked suddenly and said something in Turkish that sounded very like a curse. The narrow street they were travelling along was blocked ahead by two cars which had met head on and both drivers were refusing to give way.

Frankie had slipped her shoe back on when her threat of violence seemed to have no effect. Now, clutching her precious rugs to her, she twisted the car door handle and was out of the taxi before Dr Schmidt could grab her. She ran down an alley far too narrow for a car to negotiate, dreading the sound of footsteps in pursuit, but none came. When she reached the next thorough-fare she stopped, breathing hard, and looked desperately around, only to give a sigh of relief when she saw the hotel a few hundred yards away. Walking briskly, keeping away from the edge of the pavement and looking out for any taxis that seemed to be following her, she reached the safety of the hotel and carried her rugs up to the suite, where she found Paul already installed with a whisky and soda in his hand.

'Success!' he greeted her. 'We've made the sale. E-mails have been flying backwards and forwards between England and Turkey to confirm the agreements. We have something to celebrate tonight!'

Then he became aware of her breathless state and the bundles she was clutching to her.

'What on earth has happened to you and what have you got there?'

'I've been kidnapped and these are carpets!' she said dramatically, sinking down on the couch.

He sat up abruptly and stared at her in bewilderment.

87

'It was your Dr Schmidt,' she told him. 'He was following me and I went into a carpet shop to dodge him, but he must have waited outside and when I got into a taxi it stopped and he got in and said he wanted to talk to me.'

'But you got away?'

'I jumped out when the taxi was held up. I had visions of being kidnapped and vanishing for ever!'

'What did he say?'

'He wanted information about my work, and he seemed to be trying to bribe me.'

She didn't say anything about Schmidt's comments about matching Paul's offer. A muscle twitched in Paul's cheek.

'But you didn't tell him anything?'

'I told you, I got away.'

Paul took a deep breath, and seemed to make an effort to speak lightly.

'Well, if Wilhelm did lurk outside the carpet shop with a taxi it is the most daring thing he has ever done, and I will have a word with him about it next time I see him. Perhaps I should have explained that he isn't a James Bond sort of spy. His espionage is industrial espionage.'

'Oh!' Frankie said, her excitement somewhat dampened as she realised what he meant. 'You mean he's harmless? I didn't have to try to dodge him or threaten to hit him with my shoe? He wasn't kidnapping me?'

'I expect the taxi would have taken a long way round, but I'm sure it would have brought you here safe and sound in the long run.'

Paul pursed his lips.

'He's not completely harmless. Schmidt is very skilful at piecing together oddments of information and makes a very good living selling the result to interested parties. He can be very persistent and industrial espionage can do a lot of harm. Stolen information about products and companies' plans is worth hundreds of millions of pounds a year. LRT wouldn't like details of what it is selling and its plans for expansion in this area known too widely.'

He gave her a reassuring grin.

'You were in no danger. Bribery is more Schmidt's tactics than kidnapping.'

'He said a talk might be rewarding,' Frankie said slowly.

'You might have got a few gold chains from him, possibly even a diamond bracelet in return for your technical know-how.'

In spite of what Paul said, industrial espionage seemed rather an anticlimax after her dramatic escape, and she abandoned the subject.

'Well, I'm glad I avoided him long enough to go to the carpet shop,' she said positively, unrolling the rugs for him to see. 'Look, aren't they lovely?'

He looked at them carefully, felt them and examined the reverse.

'You've chosen well. These are good. How much did you pay?'

When she told him he raised his eyebrows.

'A very fair price.'

She picked up the rugs, ready to take them to her room.

'I just hope my grandfather likes the one I've chosen for him.'

'He's a lucky man, having a lovely rug and a very nice granddaughter. Now, can you find yet another thing to wear? I'm taking you out for dinner tonight.'

'Half an hour and I'll be transformed,' she announced.

In truth it was more than half an hour before she was finally ready, but this was their last evening in Istanbul, the deal with the Yilmaz brothers had been successfull concluded, and she was looking forward to going out with Paul. For these reasons she took great care over her appearance, applying the little make-up she needed with great care and brushing her bright hair till it shone. She was glad that Diane Beech had insisted on packing a just-in-case, knee-length shift in blue silk chiffon.

Paul, himself freshly shaved and

changed, was gazing out at the panorama when she finally emerged.

'Shall we go?' she said, and he swung round, obviously taken by surprise, and then stood looking at her for so long that she wondered what was the matter.

'What's wrong?' she said hesitantly. 'Isn't the dress suitable?'

He shook his head.

'The dress is marvellous. It's just that this is the first time I've seen you in anything that wasn't business-like or suitable for rough work. You look a dream.'

He came close and tipped up her chin with one strong finger.

'Tonight you look like a very feminine Frances,' he said solemnly.

They stood unmoving, almost touching and then his mouth came down on hers. She closed her eyes, responding to his kiss, and then abruptly he moved away and the spell was broken.

'I'm sorry, I shouldn't have done that. Put it down to the whisky,' he said.

'It's all right, Paul, I didn't mind,' she said, but he was already making briskly for the door.

'Come on, Istanbul is waiting,' he commanded her.

6

They made their way to the riverside that was never far away in Istanbul and strolled along by the water as it reflected the last colours of the evening sky and the lights that were springing up everywhere. It seemed natural to walk hand in hand, words scarcely needed to seal their companionship.

Frankie was gazing at the river and the people, looking into shop fronts and stopping sometimes to admire a building from the imperial past. Paul was aware of these, but also aware of passersby looking at the girl by his side with admiration.

'I can't believe we are here together,' he murmured finally as they leaned on a balustrade and gazed out over the rippling water. 'Why hasn't some man claimed you long ago?'

She smiled at him lazily, under the

spell of their surroundings.

'You've told me why you're still on your own. Like you, I've been attracted to a few men, but other things have come between us. Some men are put off by the idea of a woman engineer, especially when they see me in my overalls! Remember your own reaction when you first saw me? I've been too interested in my work to worry about romance, I suppose. There was one man I liked a lot, and he seemed to like me. He asked me out a few times. Then one evening he took me for a drive and the car broke down, in the middle of town, incidentally. He couldn't fix it, so I did, and that must have dented his masculine pride, because he didn't ask me out again!'

'He was a fool!'

'Not at all. When I'd got over the hurt I realised he was right. If two people are to stay together they must suit each other in many ways. Physical attraction isn't enough by itself.'

Paul wondered if he was being given

a gentle warning and shifted uneasily.

'Let's walk on. You'll get cold if you stand here much longer.'

They resumed their progress along the gentle curve of the waterside until Paul came to the area he knew and steered her gently towards a restaurant where they were welcomed and installed at a table by the window.

'Will you trust me to order?' Paul queried, and was answered by a nod.

He discussed the menu for some time with the waiter, who eventually went off to place their order and rapidly returned with a bottle of wine which he opened with a flourish. It was excellent, dry but with an elusive hint of flowers. The food when it came was a succession of small dishes that tempted the appetite without overwhelming it. Aubergines cooked with tomatoes, various salads, savoury little titbits, preceded a fish dish that was presented with some ceremony and eaten with relish.

Afterwards, Frankie reluctantly had

to reject the syrupy sweetmeats offered in favour of fresh fruit. It was growing late by the time they had finished the leisurely meal, but they were in no hurry to end their last evening in Istanbul.

'It seems impossible that by this time tomorrow we'll be back in England.' Frankie sighed. 'I know that to you it's been just one more business trip, but for me it's been an experience I shall never forget. Thanks to you I've seen Istanbul, and you've helped me overcome my fear of flying. There are a lot of places I plan to see now.'

'I think I shall remember this particular trip for a long time, and for special reasons,' he responded with meaning.

Frankie was aware of the implications of what he said, but she looked at him a little sadly.

'We're only here together because of the Yilmaz brothers and LRT. We may never meet again after tomorrow. You'll go back to London and flying round the world, and I'll go back to Yorkshire and Pickard's.'

He shook his head.

'We'll see each other again,' he said positively, and she was surprised at his certainty.

'I want to see you again, anyway,' he assured her, 'but there are other things that are likely to bring us together. Things may change for both of us in the near future.'

He leaned forward confidentially.

'There is something I think you ought to know, something that may make a big difference to your life. I suppose I've hinted at this once or twice, but I think I can tell you because it will be public knowledge in a few days. LRT is going to take over Pickard's.'

He sat back, obviously expecting surprise, interest, curiosity, but Frankie could only gaze at him in mute horror as the full meaning of what he said sank in.

'What's the matter?' he asked her a

little impatiently. 'Pickard's couldn't go on as it has been doing for much longer. Fred Pickard must retire soon for his own sake as well as for the good of the company. He's built up a fine firm, but he's too old now, running out of energy and getting old-fashioned, reluctant to face the changes that have to be made to keep up with modern developments.'

By now Frankie had recovered her voice.

'You mean LRT wants to wipe Pickard's out of existence, to reduce it to just a little part of their big machine?'

He looked taken aback at this, and shook his head in exasperation.

'You may not know it, but LRT takes nearly all Pickard's production already. It's almost integrated with us now. All we've got to do is replace Fred Pickard.'

'Nonsense! Mr Pickard always said he'd never become totally dependent on any firm.'

'He may have said that in the past,

but he's let it happen now. Two years ago Pickard's was struggling to survive. It was only a big order from LRT that saved the firm, and he's been relying on us since.'

Frankie frantically tried to remember if she had known anything about that crisis, but she had always concentrated on development and production and knew little about where the goods were sold.

'You talk about just replacing him as if it was unimportant, but it will kill Fred Pickard to give up the firm he founded,' she insisted, forgetting her own uneasiness about her grandfather's age, remembering only his enthusiasm for the firm he had created.

'He's seventy-four. He can't go on much longer.'

'He's fit and capable enough to go on for another ten years.'

'He can spend those years enjoying himself. Your grandfather will get a good price for his shares.'

His face suddenly became expressionless as he realised what he had said while Frankie stared at him in shock.

'How long have you known that Fred Pickard is my grandfather?' she said quietly.

He bit his lip and looked at her ruefully.

'LRT knew he had a granddaughter who worked for the firm as well as holding shares in it. It was only when Fred Pickard said something when I telephoned him that I realised you must be the granddaughter. I didn't mention it because you obviously didn't want it known.'

He was leaning forward, bringing the whole power of his personality to bear persuasively.

'It will be a good deal for your grandfather, for the firm, and for you. I know you hold thirty per cent of the shares. Once the deal is completed you will be a rich woman, Frankie.'

She remembered the way his eyes had lingered on the treasures of the Topkapi Palace, how enviously he had spoken of the rich men he had encountered, and shivered as she recalled his kiss. Was this romantic evening, the whole trip to Istanbul, just an attempt to gain a rich wife? Oblivious of her thoughts, he was continuing with his arguments.

'Did you hope to take over the firm one day?'

She shook her head fiercely.

'I'm not a manager, but the firm is my grandfather's whole life. If you take that away from him he'll just sit around wondering what to do with the rest of his life. The money won't mean anything to him. As you've found out, I own the shares that he gave to my mother, and I'll do all I can to stop this take-over.'

The glamour of the early part of the evening had vanished, completely forgotten, and Paul's voice was cold.

'Very dramatic! But your minority holding won't stop it going through. See sense. LRT wants control over the production of components. If Pickard's did stay independent, LRT would probably decide to form its own unit, and that would mean the end of Pickard's anyway, and of your cosy little job in the family firm.'

Her face reddened at the implication. She knew that she had been appointed on merit, but also knew that inevitably there had been murmurs even within Pickard's. Abruptly she stood up.

'I want to go back to the hotel, now!'

Now Paul was also on his feet for a final appeal.

'Frankie, you're jumping to conclusions again! Why don't you wait and see how Fred Pickard feels?'

'I'm his granddaughter and I know how he feels. I shall help him fight LRT! It's about time you realised that there are more important things than business and profit. No wonder no woman ever stayed with you!'

His lips tightened. A hovering waiter was beckoned and ordered to produce the bill. Very soon they were out of the restaurant and heading back to the hotel. Unlike their earlier progress they were marching along rapidly, faces set, with a marked distance between them. They stood silent and apart in the lift, and when Paul opened the door of the suite Frankie stalked past him, eager to reach her bedroom, but he caught her arm and swung her round to face him, seizing her above the elbows.

'Frankie, don't let it end like this!' he whispered.

His voice had dropped, becoming tender and intimate.

'We've become friends, haven't we? We could go on to become closer. Don't let an old man who should have given up his firm long ago come between us.'

He drew her closer till their bodies were almost touching, but she pulled away, fighting against his grip.

'Was it really a mistake when we were given a suite instead of two separate rooms?' she threw at him. 'Or did you plan to use your charm on the naïve Yorkshire girl? Did you hope to get a rich wife out of this trip as well as a big sale? Then you could have started your own firm with my money!'

He let go of her abruptly and she almost ran to her bedroom, slamming the door behind her and turning the key. She plumped down miserably on the edge of her bed, and thought about what he had told her. If he was correct, then there was nothing she could do with her minority shareholding to stop LRT incorporating Pickard's in its giant organisation. If they threatened to take their custom away from Pickard's and ruin the business, her grandfather would have to sell them his beloved firm, his reason for living, or face ruin for himself and disaster for those who worked for him.

In all honesty, few other people would suffer. She could not imagine Diane Beech as anything but her grandfather's secretary, so she would probably retire, but Frankie was sadly aware that there were many aspects of the small firm that would benefit from investment, and some out-of-date practices that hindered its full efficiency. John Seeley had frequently pointed them out. A new manager who had the energy to inspect the working areas instead of sitting in his comfortable office and issuing orders through Miss Beech, as her grandfather tended to do, would soon put things in order.

She sighed heavily before standing up to take off her dress and start packing. Her suitcase was soon ready. That done, she went to bed and then lay miserably awake a long time, reluctant to acknowledge that she was mourning not only the destruction of her grandfather's little world but also the loss of the relationship that she had believed that she and Paul Hillwood had begun to share.

At twenty-five she was ready for love, and sighed as she remembered that one kiss, and the way he had looked at her. No-one had excited her in quite that way before. Well, she would have to forget the kiss. Paul Hillwood was part of the huge, faceless business empire that wanted to get rid of her grandfather, and her loyalty was to the old man who had reared her, whose blood she shared.

She was awake, heavy-eyed and miserable, some time before her alarm sounded, and had plenty of time to finish her packing before Paul knocked briefly and summoned her to breakfast, an almost silent meal where she picked reluctantly at a little food. They were ready, waiting in the lobby when the taxi arrived, with nothing that they could say to each other.

Once the check-in formalities at the airport were complete, Frankie found it impossible to remain sitting by the tight-lipped and wordless Paul, and wandered round the departure area. She knew that the day before she would have been filled with curiosity, examining everything with enthusiasm, but now it was an effort to summon up any interest. She bought some Turkish Delight and chestnuts in syrup as presents for her grandfather and Miss

Beech, and remembered to add some for John Seeley.

Then there was nothing to do but wait till they were summoned to board their aircraft. Once again the ritual of instruction and take-off was gone through and as the plane taxied along the runway, Frankie felt herself once again growing tense and nervous. She clenched her fists in her lap and Paul Hillwood must have noticed this, for he tentatively held out his hand to her. She turned her head away, deliberately ignoring this offer of comfort. Rebuffed, he withdrew it sharply.

The plane was not full, and once they were in the air, he had a word with a stewardess and then moved to an empty pair of seats where he spent the flight deep in paperwork, ignoring Frankie until the uneventful landing at Manchester. It was only as they were waiting by the carousel for their luggage that he approached her again.

'I assume that you are being met, or

that you are taking a taxi to your home. I'm transferring to a flight to London, so this is goodbye. I doubt now if we shall see each other again.'

She felt a pang of distress. Suddenly she wanted to thank him for all his help, for showing her Istanbul. It wasn't his fault that LRT was going to destroy her grandfather's life. Before she could speak, however, he went on formally.

'Thank you for your assistance with our negotiations. In spite of your reaction to the news of the take-over, I shall recommend that LRT retains your services if you are willing to stay.'

Before she could reply, he had scooped his luggage off the carousel, bowed his head to her, and walked away without hesitation. She would have followed him, said goodbye more fully, if her own suitcase had not come into sight at that moment. By the time she had secured it Paul Hillwood had vanished, and all she could do was make her way out to where John Seeley was waiting to drive her home.

7

John took Frankie's suitcase from her and heaved it on to the back seat, peering a little anxiously at her drawn face.

'A good trip?' he enquired.

She shrugged and sank into the passenger seat.

'It had its good and bad bits, John, but don't ask me about it at the moment because I'm tired out with travelling.'

He did not look as if this explanation satisfied him completely as he drove them out of the airport.

'Everything's fine at home,' he told her. 'There was a bit of a gale on Wednesday that brought down a few branches on the apple trees, but otherwise there's nothing to report.'

She lay back in the passenger seat and closed her eyes. How comforting it was to come back home, where the most exciting event was a few twigs blown off the trees! Now she had two whole days to rest and gather the strength to face her grandfather and his problems on Monday. She wondered if he knew yet that the predatory jaws of LRT were open, ready to engulf his little firm.

When they pulled up outside the cottages she opened her eyes and managed to smile at John gratefully.

'Thank you for meeting me and bringing me home, John.'

'You know I'm always glad to help,' he responded, carrying her suitcase up the path and opening her front door with the spare key he kept for her. 'I came in earlier and turned the heating on, so it's nice and warm after all those foreign places.'

Left alone, Frankie made herself some tea but even home was unable to erase the memory of Paul and there were sudden tears in her eyes as she recalled the growing warmth between them and the frosty conclusion that had ruined it. Well, Paul Hillwood was one of the enemy, and she would not be seeing him again anyway.

She unpacked, hanging up the blue dress carefully. She stroked it a little wistfully, then thrust it to the back of her wardrobe. Afterwards, a long shower washed away the last traces of Istanbul. The tension of the flight after the restless night had indeed left her tired and she slept deeply. In the morning she was back into her familiar sweatshirt and overalls, tidying up the patch of garden behind the cottage. She broke off to take her small gifts to John and found him just about to set off on his weekly visit to his father who was now none too happily installed in a comfortable nursing home in Bradford which absorbed a large part of John's salary.

'What about that chap you went with?' John asked her after he had thanked her briefly for her gifts. 'How did you get on with him?'

Frankie smiled wryly.

'He was as chilly at the end as he was at the beginning,' she told him, aware that though the statement was true it left out some important facts!

John roared off on his motorbike before she could broach the subject that dominated her thoughts, and she hoped to be able to discuss the threatened take-over by LRT with him on the Sunday. He could tell her how the rest of the staff might view it. But there was no sign of life in the neighbouring cottage on Sunday so, wondering what had happened to John, she devoted the day to the old Aston Martin. The combination of mechanical knowledge and the sheer physical effort of putting it into practice was satisfying and kept her mind off the coming day, but in the evening she brooded on the take-over, wondering if there was anything she could do. Even if her thirty per cent of the shares couldn't stop it, she would make sure that she was a very awkward minority owner.

She was at the works early the next morning, aware that her grandfather would be expecting a report on her trip to Istanbul, and by nine-thirty she was in the outer office, presenting Diane Beech with some exotic goodies. The secretary accepted them with pleasure, but though Frankie waited expectantly she made no mention of any sensational developments while the girl had been away. So Fred Pickard didn't know yet! She went in to see him and was greeted with a beaming smile and a hug.

'How did it go?' he asked anxiously.

'Very well. We got the order.'

'I'm not talking about the business affairs. What about flying?'

With an effort she recalled her fear at the beginning of the week.

'I was a bit nervous about take-off and landing, but otherwise I quite enjoyed it. I loved looking down at all the landscapes we flew over.'

His anxious look vanished and he gave a sigh of heartfelt relief.

'Well, that's a good thing. You've got

the whole world to explore now.'

She braced herself to break the news without further delay.

'Granddad, there's something I've got to tell you. LRT is planning to take over the firm.'

His face was a picture of consternation and annoyance and he thumped his desk with his clenched fists.

'How did you hear that? I wanted to tell you myself!'

Frankie's mouth fell open and she stared at him.

'You knew? How are you going to stop them? Can you fight it?'

Now it was his time to stare.

'Fight it? Stop it? Why should I do that? I was the one who went to them and suggested it.'

She looked at him in disbelief.

'But this is your firm! You've spent your whole working life here.'

'Aye, and now I'm seventy-four and I've had enough. I want to enjoy the time I've got left, not spend it worrying about orders and production problems, or making all the changes that are needed to bring the firm up-to-date. LRT and I have come to a very good arrangement.'

'How long has this been going on?'

'Oh, we finalised the deal about ten days ago.'

Ten days. If only she had known, what a difference it would have made to her response to Paul Hillwood!

'You might have told me,' she said bitterly.

'You? Why should I bother you with the details until it was all settled? You'll bring some lucky man a good dowry with what you'll get for your shares, incidentally.'

'I said you should have told her, Fred,' Diane Beech said reprovingly, having just come in with the tea tray.

Fred Pickard gave her an indignant glare.

'It was going to be a nice surprise for her until someone let the cat out of the bag. I suppose it was that Paul Hillwood.'

Frankie turned to the secretary.

'What are you going to do, Diane? I can't imagine you staying here without my grandfather.'

Fred Pickard answered triumphantly for Miss Beech.

'Don't worry about Diane. She and I are going to get married and spend our honeymoon in Normandy!'

This was far too much to be taken in quickly! Frankie pushed back her chair and waved away the teacup she was being offered.

'No thanks, I think I'll just go back to my office and think about all this.'

It was there that Diane Beech found her half-an-hour later. As she opened the door Frankie sprang to her feet guiltily.

'Diane! Come on in. I want to say I'm sorry for the way I behaved in Granddad's office. I didn't even congratulate the two of you on your engagement!'

Diane Beech's look was full of understanding.

'It must all be a shock to you. I mean, the firm going to LRT and the fact that I'm going to be your step-grandmother!'

'I'm very glad about that!' Frankie said warmly. 'Granddad should have married you years ago.'

Diane Beech laughed.

'I could have married him any time during the past twenty years if I'd said the word,' she confided. 'But he would never have let me go on working then. He would have expected me to stay in that great empty house of his and be what he would consider a good wife. As his secretary I shared his life. Now he's leaving the firm at last, we can spend our remaining time together as man and wife.'

Frankie gave her a spontaneous kiss, but then her face fell.

'I wish he'd told me about the take-over, though! After all, it's a family firm and I own nearly a third.'

Diane made sympathetic noises, but Frankie was aware that she did not see it as a very important matter.

'Fred wanted to tell you when absolutely everything had been settled. He said it wouldn't make much difference to you, apart from the money you'll get. You didn't want to run the firm yourself, did you? You've always made it clear you weren't interested in the management side,' she pointed out.

When Diane had gone back to Fred Pickard, Frankie put in some hard thinking. Ruefully she concluded that although her grandfather paid lip-service to the idea of sexual equality, to him she was really just his granddaughter, showing off her cleverness by playing with electronics while waiting for a suitable husband to come along. His comment about her dowry proved this.

Finally she forced herself to think of Paul, and reluctantly acknowledged that she had made a fool of herself. Maybe it had not been her fault due to being kept in ignorance, but the fact remained that while she had been furiously reproaching him for being part of a plot to ruin her grandfather's life, it had been her grandfather himself who had made the first move to get rid of Pickard's.

She went to find John Seeley and tell him about the success of the mission to Istanbul. Unusually, his motorbike had not been in its usual place when she arrived, but she found him in his chair in front of the computer, brooding, with folded arms, on his next move. He looked up sharply as she came in.

'Hello, Frankie. I'm sorry I was late but my father isn't very well at the moment so I've spent the last two nights at the nursing home. Are you ready to tell me now how Istanbul was?'

She perched on the edge of his neatly-arranged desk.

'It all went very well. We got the order, and I was told, incidentally, that LRT thinks highly of our work.'

'So they should. I thought you said there were some bad bits?'

'That was personal, nothing to do with work,' she returned hastily.

There was a flicker of interest in his eyes, but when she did not offer any further information his gaze returned to the screen in front of him, as though he was politely waiting for her to leave before he touched the keyboard. Frankie, however, was still trying to adjust herself to different viewpoints on her small world. She remembered what Paul Hillwood had said to her about her place in the firm.

'John,' she suddenly blurted out, 'when we were both interviewed for my job, how did you feel when I got it?'

He showed no surprise, considering the question for some time.

'It was what I expected,' he said finally, but as she started to relax he went on. 'I think as electronic engineers, there isn't much to choose between us, but as soon as I found out who you were I knew you'd get the job. After all, blood's thicker than water.'

She stared at him. She had worked closely with him so long, and never realised that this was what he thought.

'Did you really believe that being related to Fred Pickard helped? Did you resent that?'

He gave a short laugh.

'What was the use? I did wish my dad had his own firm, but I still ended up with a good job.'

But he couldn't have stifled all the resentment, she knew. There had been those times when his ideas had been better, when he had pointed out her errors. Surely then he must have thought that he should have her job? Now he was tapping uneasily on the desk top.

'While we're talking about this, incidentally, I think I should tell you now that if my father dies, and the doctors don't give him much longer, I'll start applying for other jobs. There's a big firm which has been advertising for an electronic engineer to manage a department, and I've sent for details.'

Frankie felt that her world was crumbling about her. Her grandfather and Diane Beech would soon be leaving the firm, and now John, too, wanted to leave! She realised how much she had come to depend on him, and how much difficult her own working life would be without his solid support.

'But you've been here ever since you started work. There have been other jobs advertised in the past. Why now?'

He shrugged, avoiding her eyes.

'While my father is alive I have to stay near him in Bradford, but when he's gone I'll have much more freedom.'

'If it's a question of money ... ' Frankie began, and then stopped.

LRT would be making such decisions soon, not her grandfather, but John was shaking his head firmly.

'I'm tired of always being second in command, Frankie.'

Now he look at her directly.

'I think the final straw was this trip to Istanbul. When I was a little lad the library was throwing out some old books and I was given that guide book I lent you, and I fell in love with the pictures of Istanbul. Ever since then

I've dreamed of going there. Then, when someone from Pickard's is asked to go, you are the automatic choice. To you it wasn't even something special!'

His voice showed uncharacteristic strength of feeling, and she felt shaken. Then he sighed, and shrugged.

'I'd have moved on somewhere else eventually, I suppose, and someday I'll get to Istanbul, but I'm half-scared I'll be disappointed. Is it so wonderful or just another big city?'

Frankie thought of the skyline pierced with domes and minarets, recalling the walk along by the Golden Horn, hand-in-hand with Paul.

'It's one of the most romantic places in the world,' she said warmly. 'Go there. Istanbul won't disappoint you!'

They smiled at each other in a rare moment of personal togetherness and then Frankie thought of something. LRT was a very big concern with room for more than one electronics department, and they were already aware of John Seeley's worth.

'Don't be in too much of a hurry to move,' she warned him. 'I can't give you any details, but there may be big changes here soon.'

He raised his eyebrows, then nodded slowly as though some suspicion had been confirmed.

'Really? Well, there have been rumours. I'll apply for this other job anyway, but if it's offered to me I'll think before I accept it.'

He rose.

'While you're here, why don't we go and see how they are getting on with the new project?'

In the workshop, the craftsmen were delicately putting the finishing touches to a new part. Normally Frankie would have been absorbed in the details of its fashioning, but today she felt exhausted, unable to concentrate. If John Seeley had realised that something was about to happen to the firm, why hadn't she? Perhaps she had been too cosy in her little world to consider the possibility of change.

'I think I might take the rest of the day off,' she remarked to John as they turned to leave, and overheard one of the workmen mutter, 'It's all right for some,' to his companion.

She ignored the remark, but was uneasily aware of its truth. No other employee at Pickard's would be able to decide to take time off just because they felt like it. She was the privileged granddaughter. To compensate for her feeling of guilt, in fact, she stayed late, working hard to deal with the back-log of work that had accumulated while she was away. During the day she got a message from her grandfather asking her to join him and Diane for dinner at his house. His invitations amounted to commands, so although she was desperate to go home and think in quiet about all that she had learned that day, she drove to his house straight from work.

Diane received her as the acknowledged hostess, filling the rôle easily. During the meal, Frankie observed the couple through new eyes. It was

126

obvious that they were regarding their coming married life as the start to a new and exciting period in their lives, not by any manner of means as a few twilight years. They revealed that they intended to spend most of the year in France in the future, and her grandfather even spoke casually about the possibility of selling the house and buying a flat somewhere for their time in England. Frankie could hardly believe her ears. The big, Victorian mansion had always been his home, just as his office at Pickard's had always been his working environment, and she found it difficult to imagine him enjoying his retirement anywhere else.

Grimly she acknowledged to herself that just as she had remained essentially a little girl to her grandfather, so to her he had been an unchanging elder figure, not a human being who could develop and take on new challenges even in his later years. After dinner, the conversation changed to business matters. Remembering John Seeley, she asked when the workers were going to be told about the take-over.

'When it's all signed and binding,' Fred Pickard announced.

'When will that be?'

'Next week. Diane and I are going down on Tuesday to LRT's main offices in London, and I'll be signing the final agreement on Wednesday.'

Paul Hillwood was based in London! Frankie's eyes took on an eager look.

'Can I come, too? I'd like a trip to London, and I wouldn't mind seeing the man who came with me to Istanbul, if he's there. We got on surprisingly well, most of the time!'

Diane looked at her with interest.

'I meant to ask you about him, but so much has been happening that I forgot. He seemed a very pleasant young man when we spoke on the telephone.'

Frankie nodded her agreement.

'I would like to see him again.'

'Then you shall,' Diane Beech declared. 'Fred, she's coming with us!'

8

Frankie began to cherish a little flicker of hope. Perhaps, as Paul Hillwood had been involved in the recent sales trip to Istanbul, he might be invited to the meeting in London when the take-over papers for Pickard's were to be signed.

But before she went to London there was one unhappy episode. After John had mentioned his guide to Istanbul, Frankie had spent some time searching desperately for it, only to be forced to admit to herself in the end that she had lost it. She remembered picking it up when she left the carpet shop. She must have left it in the taxi when she left it so unexpectedly!

The following evening John knocked on the door.

'I just thought I'd call for my guide book,' he explained. 'I hope you found it useful.'

Frankie gulped.

'I did,' she stammered. 'I took it with me when I wanted to look round Istanbul. Unfortunately, I left it in a taxi.'

He stared at her disbelievingly.

'You've lost my book? Left it in a taxi?'

She nodded unhappily and guiltily tried to defend herself.

'I didn't know how much it meant to you. You shouldn't have lent it to me if it was so important.'

He looked at her with a strange expression on his normally placid face.

'After all, it was only a guide book. I'll get you another one.'

There was no point in continuing. John had turned on his heel and left the cottage, slamming the door.

Frankie was surprised by the way that her life fell back into its usual routine during the next few days, with one exception. She and John Seeley worked away in their own little area but contact was coldly formal on his side, no matter how she tried to break down the barrier he had created. Otherwise at work, nothing seemed to have changed.

She grew almost indignant that the world was ignoring the demolition of her own little universe. Then she grew annoyed with herself. How was she suffering? Her inheritance from her parents in addition to her comfortable salary meant she was financially secure. She would probably be kept on at Pickard's, so she would not even have to leave her cottage or look for work. No, she scolded herself, her trouble was that she had finally had to wake up and realise that her grandfather and Miss Beech did not see her as the only thing of interest in their world, and that it was probably not just her superior brain which had brought her professional success. And it was her fault that she had lost John's prized childhood possession.

Sitting disconsolately by the fire late one night she finally admitted to herself that much of her misery was due to the break-up of her relationship with Paul Hillwood. It did not matter that she had only known him a few days. She remembered the way his eyes crinkled at the corners when he was amused, the touch of his hand on hers, the clear lines of his mouth, and its warmth on hers. She felt she must be in love, and no matter how much she blamed her grandfather for keeping her in ignorance about his negotiations with LRT, her hot-headed reaction to the news was what had caused the split between them.

She was not quite sure what she hoped to achieve on the visit to London. She owed Paul an apology, at least. Perhaps she would get a chance to explain, and if she could make him understand how she had felt it was possible they could resume their friendship. At least she might see him once more, and with this in mind she was glad to close her cottage door behind her and forget her breach with John Seeley as she set out for London.

She took care over her appearance before the meeting, and her grey suit and heavy cream silk blouse enhanced her colouring. Her grandfather was in a jovial mood. In a few hours he would be a rich man and free at last from the pressures of running his firm, free to marry Diane Beech and live the rest of his life as he pleased. Diane herself was obviously equally happy, though more self-contained. The years as a secretary would soon be behind her, and she, too, was looking forward to her new life with the man she had loved for so long.

'Of course, it will be a few weeks yet before I can shake the dust of the old firm off my feet,' Fred Pickard said. 'I will tell the employees myself on Friday, and then whoever LRT send to take over will work alongside me till he knows all the ropes. When he's ready, Diane and I can take off, and then he can do what he likes with the firm as far as I'm concerned. I'll have my money.'

Frankie still found it difficult to accept that her grandfather could part with his life's work so easily, but Diane Beech had assured her that he was speaking the truth.

'He's been there a long time, and at his age it is becoming a burden. At one time he intended to hand it over to your parents when he reached sixty. We had all our plans made, but when they were killed there was no-one to take over and he felt he had to carry on.'

So over the long years he had continued to do his duty, postponing his plans, while the woman he loved continued by his side as his secretary but not his wife. Frankie did not dare ask if he had been hoping during those years that she herself would show an interest in managing the firm. Had he gone on working for her sake only to be disappointed?

Then she looked at her two companions, seeing how happy and fulfilled they were together, and told herself that whatever their plans had been originally, those past years had not been wasted.

As her grandfather struggled out of the taxi outside the administrative headquarters of LRT, Frankie stood on the pavement and gazed up at the smooth, modern lines of the tall building and reflected that Pickard's would be like a minnow being swallowed by a whale, but no matter how small a catch they might be they were received with great politeness on the steps of the building and escorted to the chairman's office, where a number of people were waiting for them.

Paul Hillwood was nowhere to be seen, however.

The negotiations had all taken place, and all that remained was for the final documents to be signed. This was done with full ceremony, and then sherry was produced to mark the occasion. As the meeting broke up into small groups, Frankie found herself talking to one of the directors.

'I have already had dealings with LRT,' she reminded him. 'I went to Istanbul very recently with one of your salesmen, Paul Hillwood. I thought he might be here today. He took great care of me and I wouldn't mind seeing him again to thank him.'

The director smiled politely.

'I'm afraid he's been away. We are expecting him soon, and in fact we are very eager to see him ourselves.'

Frankie's heart sank. So the trip had been wasted as far as seeing Paul was concerned! She continued to chat, but disappointment clutched her heart. Finally it was time to disperse. Fred Pickard had promised Diane and Frankie lunch at one of the top restaurants in London as a celebration, and he was eager to get away, almost hustling the two women out of the room. A taxi was waiting for them, but as they started down the steps towards it another drew up behind it. Frankie stopped abruptly at the sight of Paul Hillwood getting out of it, and when he looked up and saw her standing there he, too, halted. For a second or two they stared at each other, and then his long legs mounted the steps until he stood facing her.

'I thought you were away on another trip,' Frankie blurted out.

'I was till late last night,' he responded.

Both of them were aware that they were simply making polite noises. There was so much that Frankie wanted to say that she found it difficult to sort out her words. As she hesitated, her grandfather called from the waiting taxi, urging her to hurry up. Paul glanced at the elderly man.

'That's my grandfather, Fred Pickard,' Frankie told him hastily. 'He's just signed the documents for the transfer of the firm.'

Paul raised his eyebrows.

'He was the one who suggested the take-over,' she said flatly. 'I know that now.'

As he looked at her with sudden alertness she laid a hand on his arm.

'I'm sorry for what I said in Istanbul,' she told him. 'My only excuse is that he kept me in ignorance.'

Before he could reply, Diane Beech hurried back up the steps and touched her on the arm.

'Please, come on,' she told her. 'Fred's getting very impatient.'

Frankie had no alternative but to descend the steps towards the taxi, almost stumbling as she looked back at Paul Hillwood. Her last glimpse of him as they drove away was of him standing on the steps, his gaze following their taxi.

The lunch was everything that her grandfather had promised, so splendid that even Frankie, in spite of her preoccupation, was able to enthuse enough about it to satisfy him. When it finally drew to a close he turned to her, smiling.

'I'm taking Diane on a little shopping expedition now,' he announced. 'It's one we'd like to do on our own. Can you amuse yourself for a couple of hours?'

'Of course,' she said brightly. 'I'm not

a little girl who has to be looked after all the time now, Granddad.'

He gave her a searching look.

'Maybe we're trying to tell each other something,' he said gruffly as Diane looked from one to the other.

It was a couple of hours later when there was a knock on the door of Frankie's hotel room. Diane entered, holding out her left hand. A large diamond glittered on her engagement finger. Frankie exclaimed in delight.

'It's gorgeous! Is this the shopping you wanted to do?'

Diane nodded, for once excited and flustered.

'Fred was just like a young man. He insisted on taking me to Bond Street, and it took ages to choose, because every time I said I liked one he insisted that I should have a bigger diamond. This one's so big I'm almost scared to wear it!'

'It's beautiful and you deserve it,' Frankie said sincerely. 'Wear it with pride. It shows how much he loves you.'

Diane blushed, turning the ring this way and that to see how the many facets of the diamond glittered.

'Some day someone will buy a ring like this for you,' she said.

'It doesn't look very likely at the moment,' Frankie said forlornly.

Some note in her voice registered with Diane, who temporarily forgot her ring and looked at Frankie sharply.

'What's the matter, my love? All the way down here yesterday you seemed tense, and you were the same this morning, as if you were expecting something to happen. Then, once we'd left LRT you changed, as if something had disappointed you and you felt depressed.'

The older woman sat down beside Frankie and put her arm round her.

'What's the matter? Is it because the firm has gone?'

Frankie managed a brave grin.

'It's not that. I'm glad Granddad has got what he wanted, that now he is going to marry you and enjoy life in France.'

'Then what's upsetting you?'

'Everything has happened so quickly. For the first time in my life, I'm not sure what's going to happen in the future.'

Diane patted the girl comfortingly.

'You should be feeling excited, not frightened. You're young, intelligent and now you're rich. What more do you want?'

She glanced at her watch.

'I'd better get back to your grandfather before he starts to think I've run away with the ring,' she said.

Frankie looked up in alarm.

'You're not going to tell him I'm feeling miserable, are you?'

'Of course not! He'd only get upset and blame himself, and that would spoil his great day.'

She stood up, smoothing her crumpled skirt.

'Everything will be all right. Just wait and see.'

The train journey back the following morning was uneventful. Fred Pickard was inclined to fuss because Frankie was unusually quiet, but she assured him that it must have been the London air which had given her a headache, and that she would be perfectly well again as soon as they were back in Yorkshire. He turned to the subject of the meeting with the employees of Pickard's which he would hold the following day.

'Do you think they'll feel that I've let them down, that I'm going to take the money and run?' he asked anxiously.

Both women told him this was nonsense. He had shown his care for his workers in many ways over the years, and the employees would certainly remember this.

'I made sure there won't be any compulsory redundancies. Some of the older workers may feel it's time to go, that they don't want to stay when things are altered, but LRT is prepared to be generous to them. It's to their advantage to have a willing work force.'

He brooded silently for a while,

staring out of the window at the passing countryside.

'Of course,' he burst out finally, 'it will all depend on whom LRT sends to take over.'

In fact the meeting went extremely well. It seemed to Frankie that she had been the only one, shut away in her little domain, who had not been aware that changes were in the air. Most of the employees were pleased. Watching the firm's owner grow older, they had worried about their future, and were relieved that continuity had been assured.

'LRT will be sending in their own manager some time next week,' he informed them. 'There will be changes, but I can't tell you what, because he'll be the one to decide, and if he has any sense he won't be in too much of a hurry. What I can tell you is that you'll be all right. If you want to stay, you can. If you decide to leave then you won't go empty-handed.'

What Fred Pickard had not expected

was the obvious care and affection that his employees felt for him. Their congratulations to him and Diane Beech, and their spontaneous thanks for all he had done in the past, moved him almost to tears. Back in his office after the meeting, he wiped his eyes and blew his nose loudly.

'It makes me feel I've achieved something when they pay me such compliments,' he told Diane and Frankie. 'I wonder if the new man will feel the same after as many years.'

Of course there were some shocks Frankie was not prepared for during the next few weeks. She nearly stalled her car the day she drove up to the factory gates and saw that the familiar, rather battered sign proclaiming Pickard, Engineers had been replaced by a smartly-designed sign proclaiming LRT's ownership. Other changes went more smoothly. LRT sent a comfortably-built Yorkshireman named Edwards with an easy smile but shrewd eyes to prepare to take over from Fred Pickard. Within days, Fred had announced happily that he didn't have to sit there acting as nursemaid every day and had retreated to his Victorian mansion.

'Edwards knows he can always call me here if he wants to,' he told Frankie. 'And so far,' he said very contentedly, 'he hasn't called me very often.'

When Frankie had to visit his familiar office nowadays she found it difficult to accept the changes. The great desk and the leather chair were still there, but all the clutter, the photographs and other items Fred Pickard had accumulated over the years had been swept away, and a computer, something Fred Pickard had resolutely refused to master, now stood on his desk.

Mr Edwards had brought his own secretary with him, a dark-haired brunette in her late twenties who was always immaculately groomed and made-up. When Fred Pickard gave up full-time work, Diane promptly retired, stating happily that one man only needed one secretary. Frankie would have loved to talk over these changes with John Seeley, but he was rarely to be seen. His father was worse and he was spending all the time he could with him. She had asked him tentatively if he had heard anything about the job he had applied for, but he had only shaken his head and muttered that he'd changed his mind about that.

Then the nursing home had called to inform him that his father was very low, and John had taken his accumulated holiday entitlement to spend it sitting by the bedside of a man who had alternately ignored him and illtreated him all his life.

One evening Frankie arrived at Fred Pickard's mansion in response to a summons from her grandfather. Diane ushered her into the drawing-room where Fred was waiting by a roaring fire.

'Grandfather,' she said suspiciously after kissing him, 'what are you up to now?'

Fred Pickard patted her.

'Wait for Diane,' he ordered her.

When Diane entered it was with a tall green bottle and three glasses. Expertly she twisted until the cork popped and the champagne foamed out to be caught in the glasses. Solemnly Diane gave a full glass to each of them, and Fred Pickard stood up, holding his aloft.

'A toast,' he announced. 'Let us drink to our wedding, tomorrow morning.'

Frankie choked and nearly spilled her champagne.

'It's true, Frances,' Diane assured her. 'We decided that as everything is going so easily at the factory that we would get married now, spend a week in London for our honeymoon, and then come back here for our first Christmas together.'

Frankie stared at them.

'Tomorrow! Nobody said anything to me at work!'

'Nobody knows, and you are not to tell them. It's going to be a very quiet wedding at the registry office, just the two of us and you. No fuss.'

Frankie looked at them with disbelief, but they were smiling happily, as excited as teenagers with their plans.

Next day, she arrived at the registry office a little before the couple, and watched as Diane's little red car drew up and Fred Pickard proudly assisted his bride into the building. Diane looked elegantly beautiful in dark gold silk with an extravagant and very becoming hat.

Frankie watched them during the brief ceremony. The bride and groom shone with happiness, all their attention focused on each other, and she found herself blinking back joyful tears. When they were man and wife she kissed them warmly.

'Greetings, Grandmother. You're a very lucky man, Fred Pickard.'

The gold silk was not suitable for a car journey, so Diane disappeared into a cloakroom to change into something more practical. Fred watched her go as if he could not bear to have her out of his sight, then sat down to wait with Frankie.

'You know,' he confided in her, 'I loved your grandmother, my first wife, but she died forty years ago. Work at the firm kept me occupied, but I was often a very lonely man until Diane came along. We suit each other. I don't know how long we'll have together, but I do know that we will be happy while we can.'

Frankie put her arms round him.

'Have I ever told you how grateful I am for all you've done for me? Take my love and best wishes with you.'

He held her awkwardly.

'At twenty-five, it's time you found someone yourself. I'd like to see some great-grandchildren.'

Diane was back soon, and they were ready to leave. Obviously they were glad that Frankie was there to share their happiness.

'We'll see you for Christmas,' Diane said as they were getting into the car, and Frankie assured them she would be there and smiled bravely, waving until the car was out of sight.

Standing on the pavement, she felt very lonely indeed. Her grandfather was right, of course. Now he and Diane had gone she needed someone she could talk to and love, just as they had each other. But who wanted her?

9

The following day she went to see Mr Edwards. News had somehow spread about the wedding and he asked her to pass on his good wishes. 'Now,' he said comfortably, settling back in the chair which she still thought of as her grandfather's, 'presumably you came to see me about work. How can I help?'

She clasped her hands together tightly in her lap, her heart thumping as she braced herself to take a big step in her life.

'I have decided to resign from my post here.'

Mr Edwards sat upright in obvious surprise.

'What?' he said, his face showing consternation. 'You're not going because of the reorganisation, are you?'

She wondered whether he was dismayed solely at the idea of losing a good employee. His next remarks clarified matters.

'If Fred Pickard's granddaughter leaves so soon after we've taken over it might look as if we're getting rid of you.'

She shook her head firmly.

'I'll make certain that that rumour isn't spread around, though I suppose in a way the take-over is responsible for my decision. It's just that now seems a good time for a new beginning. It's time for me to move on. I'm young, and I want to try other things, possibly even other countries. When everything else is changing, it seems a good time to go. If my grandfather can start a new life at seventy-four, surely I'm allowed to try something new at twenty-five? I think a change might be good for my career, but there are also personal reasons.'

'Miss Green, you know how valuable you are here!'

She looked at him earnestly.

'Thank you for saying that, but no-one is irreplaceable. I have, as I said, personal reasons for wanting to leave. I assure you I haven't made the decision lightly.'

'Then there's no more to be said,' Mr Edwards said after a thoughtful pause. 'I haven't checked your contract, but I assume you have to give a month's notice.'

'Yes, and I'll stay the full month and make sure I hand over the department without any problems.'

He nodded, making a note on a pad.

'Well, if you are determined, there's no more to be said. The firm will miss you, you know.'

Frankie drove home slowly that evening through the winter darkness, thinking that she would only travel that road for a few more weeks. Then what? The world lay before her. She had money and now she had time to do whatever pleased her, if only she knew what she wanted. Drawing up outside her home, she was suddenly delighted to see the light coming from the cottage next door. John was back! No matter how cool he had been to her recently, their friendship went back too far to be broken entirely by one incident. Surely she could talk to him, discuss her situation.

Hurriedly she locked the car and knocked on her neighbour's door. A voice bade her come in and she eagerly turned the handle and entered, only to halt abruptly on the threshold. John sat with his elbows on a table and his head resting on his hands. As she entered, he looked up reluctantly. His face was haggard and red-eyed with weariness and he was unshaven.

'My father died today,' he said without preamble.

'John, I'm so sorry.'

She hesitated. What else could she say? Could he possibly mourn his harsh and unloving parent? He gave a short laugh.

'Don't worry. I know what you're thinking. Aren't I better off without him? Won't I have some money to call my own now instead of spending it all on a man who never showed any gratitude? Perhaps. But if he didn't care for me, at least he was someone for me to care for. Now I'm alone, and I shall miss him. You won't understand that, Frances, because there have always been people to care for you and cherish you, even when your parents were killed. You've never been lonely. I've always been the outsider, watching others be happy, but at least while I had my father I wasn't completely alone.'

She was about to interrupt, to tell him how lonely she was feeling now, but he went on.

'I might as well tell you now that I've accepted a job with a new group concerned with computer design in Leeds. They want me to start immediately, and LRT has agreed to let me go.'

'Computers? I know how well you use one, but you haven't had any experience in designing them.'

He shook his head impatiently.

'You may think computers are marvellous now, but in five years' time there will be new developments you can't even imagine. It's going to offer me a whole new career.'

He lowered his head to his hands again.

'But, John, you're wrong about me. I feel so alone and I've missed you so badly,' Frankie began, and then stopped.

He didn't seem to be listening. Cautiously she approached him. Bending over him, she realised that he was fast asleep. Quietly she let herself out and softly closed the door.

When she checked early the following morning the cottage next door was already empty again. She was alone once more.

Two days later, the telephone rang at seven o'clock in the evening. Frankie was slumped on the couch in front of the television after a hard afternoon's work in the garden which had been an attempt to distract herself from her miserable mood. She managed to reach the telephone on the window-sill before the ringing stopped.

'Hello?' she said cautiously.

She didn't want suggestions from salesmen that she should replace her windows or even a friend calling up for a chat. She just wanted to be left alone to sit by herself and watch something mildly amusing and distracting on TV.

'Miss Green? Frankie?'

She straightened suddenly, eyes wide with surprise.

'This is Paul Hillwood. Is that you, Frankie?' the voice continued, doubt showing in the tone at the lack of response.

She nodded frantically, then managed to gather her wits.

'Yes. It's Frankie here. What do you want?'

She realised that this sounded ungracious as the distant voice grew even cooler.

'I'm in the area for a couple of days. After our brief meeting outside our offices I wondered if we could meet again on friendlier terms. Would you like to come out somewhere for a drink this evening? Is that possible?'

Frankie thought furiously, glancing down at her shabby clothes. She could change and meet him, of course, but that would mean a quick drink in some public place where after some polite conversation he would probably retreat to his hotel as soon as he could.

'I'm not sure,' she said doubtfully. 'My car hasn't been running too well, and I don't want to risk breaking down at night.'

Mentally she begged her little car's forgiveness!

'Could you drive out here? It would take a chunk out of your evening, I'm afraid. I know! Why don't you come here and I'll cook you dinner?'

There was a pause before he spoke again, with a hint of disbelief.

'You can cook?'

She hastily reminded herself that he had only seen her at the cottage as a mechanic apparently living on cold, baked beans. Why did people assume that if you could mend a car you couldn't cook?

'Oh, I'm sure I can find you something to eat,' she said airily.

'Oh, all right. I mean, thank you! I'll be there about eight.'

He seemed about to put the telephone down when a thought seemed to strike him.

'Incidentally, you know those processes we were dealing with in Istanbul? Now we are really part of the same firm, is there any chance you have the full details with you and could let me have them? It would save a special journey to your factory.'

'Most of the details are on my computer,' she told him, delighted that she could help him. 'I'll print them out for you.'

Frankie's hand was shaking as she put down the telephone and looked round rapidly. Food first! What had she got? Ten minutes in the little kitchen and then she raced round the sitting-room, bundling old papers and other misplaced odds and ends into a large cardboard box which she carried up to the bedroom before rapidly locating the relevant files on her computer and starting to print them out. Descending the stairs, she looked round swiftly. Firelight and wall lights cast a flattering glow on the shabby upholstery, and the small table was laid for dinner.

She glanced at the clock. Twenty-five minutes to eight! What else was there to do? John was unlikely to interrupt the evening by calling to check on the guest as he was still apparently away. She suddenly caught sight of herself in the mirror and groaned aloud as she fled up the stairs. She showered rapidly, towelling herself dry with rough haste. At least there was no doubt about what dress to wear. Diane had insisted that she buy it as soon as the shop assistant had pointed it out.

'If you ever have to say sorry to a man, that's the dress to wear while you do it,' she had pronounced.

It was creamy white, the fabric a soft,

floating chiffon over a silk base. The full skirt swayed with every movement, while the long sleeves and purity of the colour gave it an innocence that was belied by the low scoop of the neckline.

'Wear that, and a man will forgive you anything,' Diane had claimed.

Frankie hoped she would be proved right.

The knock on the door came just as she was putting on her lipstick, and she slipped her feet into simple white shoes and went downstairs to greet Paul, forcing herself to move slowly. The night was cold and wet, and he was huddled on the doorstep, his briefcase in one hand and a bottle-shaped package in the other. When Frankie opened the door the warm, glowing interior welcomed him, the dancing flames adding an element of colour to her dress. He stepped into the haven and studied her admiringly as she smiled at him, then looked round appreciatively.

'Is that for me?' she said, taking the

bottle from him. 'Please come right in and give me your coat. Would you like a drink? I have some whisky.'

He nodded hastily, shrugging off his coat, and she left him sitting on the couch while she went into the kitchen to get him a drink. The wine he had brought was a good one, she noted. Clearly he had decided that if the food was awful at least the wine would be good. She took back his whisky and a weak gin for herself and settled herself into a comfortable chair opposite him. Then, suddenly, she was overcome by shyness.

After weeks of dreaming about finding herself in just such a situation with this man, now, when she had the chance to talk freely to him, to present herself to him as an attractive woman who wanted to know him better, she could not think of any topics to discuss. He seemed equally tongue-tied, and they fell back on the usual exchange of polite remarks.

'I'm sorry to drag you out into the

country,' she told him.

'It was no trouble. Much better I come here than you break down,' he reassured her.

'I'd like to apologise again for my behaviour in Istanbul.'

'I was annoyed at the time, but later I could appreciate your eagerness to defend Mr Pickard.'

That seemed to take care of that subject. When the stilted conversation looked like drying up completely she remembered what he had asked for.

'I've got the information you wanted, by the way. It's in the blue file over there.'

His face lit up and he collected the file immediately, slipping it into his briefcase.

'You've saved me at least half a day and I'm very grateful,' he told her warmly, as if to explain his unexpected eagerness.

'Couldn't the information have been faxed or posted?'

'Head office wanted it quickly and

they thought it would be safest with me.'

He looked round, changing the subject.

'Meanwhile, I am curious to know why you are living here in this cottage when your grandfather was apparently living alone in some great house.'

She laughed.

'Because after I'd tasted freedom at university, that great house wasn't big enough for both of us! Grandfather wanted to go on running my life just as he had when I was a little girl. If a man asked me out he would have to face interrogation by Granddad when he came to pick me up, and when he took me back after the date my grandfather would be waiting up for me, and making it clear that he was not going to leave us alone together! We had some fine rows, and then Diane suggested I move into this cottage next to John, whom they knew and trusted to keep an eye on me.'

'As I've experienced!' Paul said with some feeling.

She suggested they should have dinner. He sat down at the table a little dubiously, but the smoked salmon was evidently a pleasant surprise. However, anyone could slice a lemon and butter bread. The venison steaks were another matter. She presented them grilled to perfection, complemented by buttery potatoes and fresh beans, offering him rowan jelly or mustard as accompaniments. The light, refreshing meringues and cream were a perfect finale.

As Frankie watched Paul relax, she reflected that the old proverb was right. The way to a man's good opinion, if not his heart, was definitely through his stomach. They had coffee by the fire, and Frankie nerved herself to speak before Paul could decide it was time to leave.

'I'd like to explain more about my behaviour when you told me about LRT taking over the firm,' she said quietly. 'I honestly couldn't believe that my grandfather hadn't kept me informed. I owned nearly a third of the firm, after all.'

She shook her head sadly.

'To him I was still a little girl playing at work. But then, I never saw him as anything but the immovable manager of Pickard's, instead of a man with private dreams of his own.'

'What do you plan to do now?'

'Now I want to leave. I thought to test myself somewhere else, on equal terms with others. I can afford to take a few risks.'

'On your own? What about the young man next door?'

'John Seeley? He and I work together. I'm impulsive and he's cautious so we complemented each other at Pickard's, but now we are going our separate ways.'

Now Paul was frowning, in spite of her explanation.

'Were you and he very close?'

'At work we have been, but now he's taking another job in Leeds.'

His brow smoothed magically.

'And where are you going?'

'I thought I might go abroad. Of

course, I'll probably lose contact with Pickard's, and with you. But you'll be glad to see the back of me after the way I've behaved, I expect.'

He shook his head emphatically.

'By no means! Apart from those last few hours in Istanbul, I thought we got on very well with each other. I'd like to keep in touch anyway. I'm sure we can be good friends.'

She murmured agreement while her heart sank. To be offered friendship instead of love was agony! Once again she had obviously misinterpreted how someone felt. After that kiss in Istanbul she had hoped that they had quarrelled deeply partly because they had been coming to care for each other, but clearly he saw her only as a pleasant companion for an occasional meeting. That one kiss had been the result of the blue dress and the romantic setting, to be forgotten when they returned to England.

She managed a smile.

'I'm sure you are right. We'll settle down and be good friends.'

He leaned forward and took her hand in his.

'Friends, to start with.'

There was a world of meaning in his voice and she looked at him, startled into hope, wondering if he really meant the message he was conveying.

He was looking at his watch now, apparently ready to get to his feet, but she rose before he could, reluctant to let him go before she could clarify what he meant.

'Would you like some more brandy?'

He shook his head regretfully.

'I'd better not have any more, if I'm going to drive back tonight.'

He looked into her eyes, and his message was indeed clear now. She gazed back for a long moment, and then very deliberately poured some more brandy into his glass. He gave a sharp gasp, as if he had been holding his breath while he waited for her response, and gave her a glittering smile which seemed to hold a touch of triumph.

He stood up and she waited as he moved towards her until she found herself held tightly in his arms and he was kissing her. She responded warmly and he lifted his head and looked at her intently. Then he kissed her again. At some time he must have carried her to the couch, for when she began to think clearly again they were cosily entwined on its cushions.

'I thought you saw me as just a friend,' she said breathlessly.

'What else could I say? You sat there all calm and composed as if I could have been a block of wood for all you cared!'

'But what about this dress? Didn't that have a message? Diane said I would be forgiven everything if I wore it.'

'You have been forgiven, but it's so white and pure that I was scared to touch you.'

He felt her quiver with laughter and bent his head to kiss her again.

It was at that moment that the

knocking on the door began. At first it was a firm but brief knock. This was rapidly repeated and then, as no response came, it became a thunderous, non-stop attack on the door.

'Frances!' they heard. 'It's me, John. Open this door!'

At this Frankie abruptly pushed Paul away and struggled to sit upright.

'Something must be the matter! Let me go!'

She tore herself free reluctantly and hurried to the door, flinging it open rapidly. John Seeley charged into the room like a bull and halted, facing Paul. He glared at him and then his gaze shifted to Frances, who suddenly became acutely conscious of her untidy hair and the shoes lying discarded by the couch.

'What have you come bursting in here for?' she demanded, cheeks flaming with embarrassment.

'Frankie doesn't need protecting from me, so you can leave as quickly as you came!' Paul added, now defiant.

John ignored him as he addressed Frankie.

'I thought I recognised the car as I got back! Have you given him any information — processes, products, anything?'

Frankie couldn't stop herself looking at Paul's briefcase and John pounced on it. With a shout of protest Paul tried to stop him, but the tall Yorkshire man swatted him aside casually and Paul Hillwood ended up on his back on the floor. John ripped open the briefcase and pulled out the sheaf of computer printouts. Frankie was almost crying with anger.

'What on earth are you doing? Of course I gave him the information. He wanted it for LRT!'

'He wanted it,' John said grimly, 'but not for LRT, for himself. I heard from Mr Edwards when I called him this afternoon that Hillwood was sacked last week for selling industrial secrets to a rival! This information could have been very profitable for him.'

'What nonsense!' she exclaimed.

'Look at him!'

Frankie turned to Paul Hillwood, who had groggily pulled himself upright. She was eager for him to deny the charge, but stopped at the look on his haggard face.

'It's true, isn't it?' she said softly. 'I should have remembered how important money is to you. You're a spy, like Dr Schmidt, selling secrets to the highest bidder.'

Her fingers went to her mouth, remembering his recent kisses.

'You were too greedy. You should have taken the papers and gone, but I suppose I would have been a nice little bonus tonight!'

'No!' Paul Hillwood said desperately. 'I wanted the information because I'm tired of working to make other people rich, but I do care for you, Frankie.'

Deliberately she turned her back on him. John Seeley contemptuously threw the open case at the haggard Paul.

'Get out now! There's nothing you

can say to justify yourself!'

Silently Paul Hillwood took the case and made for the door. There he half-turned and looked at Frankie who stood frozen and white-faced. Then he vanished into the dark night and they heard his car start and drive away. As the noise faded John turned to Frankie.

'Now you see what he's really like.'

All the pretty, romantic dreams had gone, been shattered. Paul Hillwood had just been using her, and she was alone again. Bitterly she faced John.

'And I shall never forgive you for being the one to show me!'

His jaw muscles tightened as she bent her head to hide the tears springing to her eyes. When she looked up again he had gone.

10

In a mixture of anger and misery Frankie cleared away the remains of the dinner, then undressed and prepared for bed, but was suddenly aware that sleep would not come for a long time. She wrapped herself in her old dressing-gown and curled up on the couch in front of the fire and thought back over the evening.

After much soul-searching she had to admit that as far as Paul Hillwood was concerned it was her pride that was hurt rather than her heart. When John had revealed Paul's real motives she had been angry at his deception, not shattered by the fact that he did not love her. She confessed to herself that she had been beguiled by him because that was what she had wanted. It had been flattering to believe that a sophisticated, experienced and attractive man

174

had desired her and it had come at a time when everyone else seemed to be abandoning her. Once the anger and hurt had faded she knew she would put the episode down to experience. There had been no lasting harm done, thanks to John.

It was when she thought of John that she felt real pain. He had saved her and LRT from the consequences of her foolishness and in return she had lashed out at him with the anger that should have been directed at Hillwood and herself. He must have gone away believing that she had genuinely cared for Paul. Well, in the morning she would go round and apologise, explain why she had reacted so badly. She would humble herself and go on explaining till she had broken down the stupid barrier of coldness that had grown between them and then she would try to rebuild their old friendship.

After she had reached this decision she felt better and went upstairs to sleep soundly, only to be woken by the sound of John's motorbike. Once again she found his cottage empty, the door shut fast, and so it remained.

Fred and Diane returned from London happy and full of plans for the future. Fred was taken aback to find that she had given in her notice to Mr Edwards and there were some spirited confrontations with Diane acting as amused referee, until he accepted unwillingly that Frankie was as free to change her life as he was. She told them she had decided to spend some time in America, visiting some college friends who had settled there, and that she planned to retain the cottage as a base.

At work, she concealed her depression behind a quiet façade, gradually handing work over to colleagues and telling everyone how eagerly she was looking forward to the future. She received a Christmas card from John telling her that his new firm had sent him on a training course to London until well into the New Year. There was no address. The only bright spot in her life was the prospect of spending Christmas Day with Fred and Diane. Both insisted on a traditional Christmas and she looked forward to being indulged in luxury and comforted by their love.

Then she received an unexpected present when the postman arrived with a small parcel with unfamiliar stamps just as she was on her way out one morning. She could hardly believe it when she found it was John Seeley's guide to Istanbul! The letter enclosed was from the hotel and simply stated that the book had been handed in with the information that Miss Green had left it behind. Frankie thrust it into her coat pocket, mentally giving thanks to the charming but unscrupulous Dr Schmidt! If only it had arrived earlier so she could have returned it to John.

When she looked out of the window on Christmas morning she saw that snow had fallen overnight and it took her some time, driving very slowly and with great care, to coax her car to her grandfather's house. It was with considerable relief that she finally drew up in front of the house. Grasping the hold-all containing her necessary luggage and the presents for Diane and Fred, she gratefully entered the warm, welcoming house. She found Fred lovingly tending the log fire in the big sitting-room, which was dominated by a large and elaborately-decorated tree.

'Merry Christmas, Granddad!' she greeted him.

He embraced her warmly.

'Merry Christmas! I knew you'd get here, though the others were beginning to wonder.'

The others? Her spirits fell slightly. Were there other guests? She had been looking forward to a quiet family party. Fred was peering past her.

'Bring it in! That's what I call a Yule log!'

Frankie turned to see to whom he was speaking. In the doorway, carrying a large, pine log, was John! Frankie was taken unawares by the joy that surged through her at the sight of his tall figure. She was being given a chance to be reconciled with him!

'John!' she greeted him. 'What a wonderful surprise!'

Encumbered by the log, he nodded in acknowledgement, his face guarded.

'Hello, Frances,' was all he said.

'Didn't you know John was coming?' Diane queried, bustling in behind him. 'When we got a card saying he would be in London on his own, Fred contacted him through the firm and invited him up here.'

'Well, we've got plenty of room here for a friend!' Fred Pickard said.

'I would have lit a fire to warm your cottage,' Frankie told John, but he shrugged.

'Why bother opening the cottage for a few days? I'll be going back to London straight from here.'

Throughout the make-shift lunch of salads and fruit, Frankie secretly eyed the familiar figure of the young man that she had known for so many years, and wondered what was different. The old sweatshirt and jeans were those he usually wore for gardening, the short blond hair and casual air of strength were the same. The difference was more subtle.

It was confidence, she realised suddenly. Through the years, she had become accustomed to John as a secondary figure, assisting others such as herself efficiently but never taking the lead. Now he was his own man, making his own choices and decisions, and the difference showed. He was no longer Fred Pickard's employee but a guest and a friend, and as the two men chatted and laughed over lunch she thought wistfully that here was the grandson Fred Pickard would have loved to have.

Lunch finished, Diane stood up authoritatively.

'Now, you two can go off for a walk while Fred and I finish getting the Christmas dinner ready.'

As John rose Frankie gave a horrified

look at the louring grey sky.

'It's cold! It's going to snow again! Can't I help you with the vegetables?'

Partly she felt genuinely reluctant to go out into the cold again, but partly she felt oddly shy at the prospect of being alone with this new John.

'Both of you are going!' Diane said firmly. 'This is my first Christmas dinner as Mrs Pickard, and Fred and I are going to get it ready.'

In the face of this, Frankie had no choice but to pull on her coat and some old boots and reluctantly leave the warm shelter of the house. Shoulders hunched, she and John set out along a road which led them away from the scattered houses towards the lonely hills. They walked in silence, a silence which lasted so long that she began to wonder if they would ever speak to each other again.

'How do you like your new firm?' she asked finally.

'I'm enjoying every minute there,' he responded.

181

'I suppose it's not a bit like Pickard's?'

He shook his head emphatically.

'Not at all like the old firm! It's new, innovative, with plenty of opportunity to do what interests me. I'm having to learn a lot very quickly, but it's exciting and stimulating.'

'When are you coming back to Yorkshire?'

He kicked idly at a tussock of wintry grass.

'In a month or two I will be back in Leeds.' He paused. 'I'll probably look for a flat there.'

'What about the cottage?' she demanded.

'I'll sell it. There's nothing to keep me there now.'

She longed to beg him to come back for her sake, but she couldn't bring herself to say so, and silence fell again as they walked on, stopping by tacit, mutual consent when they reached a high bend in the road and the wide vista of the snow-covered moors was spread out before them.

'What about you?' he enquired. 'Are you happy now? Do you still hate me because I showed you what Paul Hillwood was really like?'

She shook her head emphatically.

'I hated you for five minutes, if that. After all, you did destroy a very pretty, rose-tinted dream. Then I hated myself for being such a fool.'

After a pause he said gently, 'You haven't answered my other question. Are you happy, Frances?'

His use of her full name broke down the fragile defences of her dignity, and she found tears filling her eyes. Suddenly John's arm was round her and she was being offered a large white handkerchief.

'I didn't mean to upset you, Frances. Don't cry, please!'

The note of panic in his voice made her laugh even as the tears fell, and she gratefully took the handkerchief. He waited as she regained her composure and began to pour out the feelings she had kept to herself for so long.

'How can I be happy?' she said, stuffing the white linen fiercely into her coat pocket. 'Everything I've been used to is disappearing. Granddad and Diane will be moving to Normandy in the spring, you've already gone, and Pickard's is being changed. So far my life has followed a clear path and I've never had to look ahead and wonder what was going to happen. Even when my parents were killed, Grandfather and Diane took over. When I left them, you were near when I needed you. Now the future is as blank and depressing as those hills!'

She gestured at the grey expanse of unmarked snow before them, then turned to meet his steady, questioning gaze.

'What do you really want, Frances?'

She squared her shoulders and looked at him resolutely. It was now or never!

'I want you back. I hadn't realised how much I relied on your judgment and help at home as well as at work, how knowing that you were near me gave me comfort. Must you move to Leeds? You could easily travel there each day from Bradford.'

He didn't reply, and she turned away, ashamed of having revealed her feelings.

'It doesn't matter. I'll survive,' she whispered.

She thrust her hands into her coat pockets and suddenly felt a hard little package. Fumbling, she extracted it and held it out to him.

'Here. This belongs to you.'

Frowning, he opened the padded envelope and drew out the little book.

'My guide!'

'The hotel found it and posted it to me,' she explained as he turned it over and over lovingly.

He looked up, his face shining, and then he thrust the book into his own pocket and took her by the arms with gentle strength.

'I told you once how I dreamed of going to Istanbul, Frances. I didn't tell you then that for years I've dreamed of going there with you. I'll come back to the cottage, Frances, on one condition. You must decide whether to make my dream come true or not.'

He shook his head as she opened her mouth to speak.

'Not now! I'll come back for six months, and I won't press you for an answer. If at the end of that time you are sure you will never go to Istanbul with me, never make my dream come true, I'll leave.'

She looked at him seriously for some time, and then a small smile twitched the corner of her mouth.

'And if I'm sure, absolutely sure, before the six months is up that I would love to go anywhere in the world with you, what happens then?'

He looked at her searchingly, then his face lit up as he smiled back at her.

'When you're certain, you tell me.'

She lifted her face to him and he gave her a kiss that was as light as a snowflake.

'Now we'd better get back. Diane will never forgive us if the turkey is overcooked!'

With his arm round her shoulder, they started back along the road. At that moment a ray of light from the sinking sun found a chink in the clouds and suddenly the grey snow before them was turned to a glory of sparkling crystal.

The way ahead for them was bright and sparkling, too, and full of promise.

THE END

We do hope that you have enjoyed reading this large print book.

Did you know that all of our titles are available for purchase?

We publish a wide range of high quality large print books including:
Romances, Mysteries, Classics
General Fiction
Non Fiction and Westerns

Special interest titles available in large print are:
The Little Oxford Dictionary
Music Book, Song Book
Hymn Book, Service Book

Also available from us courtesy of Oxford University Press:
Young Readers' Dictionary
(large print edition)
Young Readers' Thesaurus
(large print edition)

For further information or a free brochure, please contact us at:
Ulverscroft Large Print Books Ltd.,
The Green, Bradgate Road, Anstey,
Leicester, LE7 7FU, England.
Tel: (00 44) **0116 236 4325**
Fax: (00 44) **0116 234 0205**

When property developer Connor Grant contracted Natalie Jensen to landscape the grounds of his large country house near Ashley in South Australia, she was ecstatic. But then she discovered he was acquiring — and ripping apart — great swathes of the town. Her own mother's house and the hall where the drama group met were two of his targets. Natalie was desperate to stop Connor's plans — but she also had to fight the powerful attraction flowing between them.

DIVIDED LOYALTIES

Phyllis Demaine

When Heather's fiancé, Adrian, is offered a wonderful job in America their future seems rosy. However, Adrian's brother, Carl, a widower, asks for Heather's help with his small, deaf son. Help which, as a speech therapist, Heather is qualified to give. But things become complicated when Carl goes abroad on business and returns with Gisel, to whom his son takes an instant dislike. This puts Heather in the position of having to choose between the boy's happiness and her own.

FINGALA, MAID OF RATHAY

Mary Cummins

On his deathbed, Sir James Mont-
gomery of Rathay asks his daughter,
Fingala, to swear that she will not
honour her marriage contract until
her brother Patrick, the new heir,
returns from serving the King.
Patrick must marry. Rathay must
not be left without a mistress. But
Patrick has fallen in love with the
Lady Catherine Gordon whom the
King, James IV, has given in
marriage to the young man who
claims to be Richard of York, one of
the princes in the Tower.

ZABILLET OF THE SNOW

Catherine Darby

For Zabillet, a young peasant girl growing up in the tiny French village of Fromage in the mid-fourteenth century, a respectable marriage is the height of her parents' ambitions for her. But life is changing. Zabillet's love for a handsome shepherd is tested when she is invited to join the La Neige household, where her mistress, Lady Petronella, has plans for her grandson, Benet. And over all broods the horror of the Great Death that claims all whom it touches.

PERILOUS JOURNEY

Caroline Joyce

After the execution of Charles I, Louisa's Royalist father considers it too dangerous for her to stay in England and arranges for her to go to the Isle of Man with Armand de la Tremouille, the nephew of the island's Royalist Governor. Their ship is boarded by Parliamentarians who plan to sail for Ireland, but a storm causes them to be shipwrecked on the Calf of Man. Magnus Stapleton, the Parliamentarian chief, becomes infatuated with Louisa, but she has fallen in love with Armand.

NEATH PORT TALBOT LIBRARY
AND INFORMATION SERVICES

No.		No.		No.		No.	
1	NOV 2008	25		49		73	2/15
2		26		50	1/14	74	
3		27		51		75	
4	3/19	28		52		76	
5		29		53		77	
6	6/14	30		54		78	
7	10/07	31		55		79	
8	1/06	32		56		80	
9		33		57		81	
10		34		58		82	5/12
11		35		59		83	
12		36		60		84	
13		37		61		85	
14	5/13	38		62		86	
15		39		63		87	
16		40		64		88	
17		41		65		89	
18		42		66		90	1/13 7/18
19		43	8/05	67		91	
20		44	9/12	68		92	
21		45	2/11	69		COMMUNITY	
22		46	8/08	70		SERVICES	
23		47		71		NPT/111	
24		48		72			

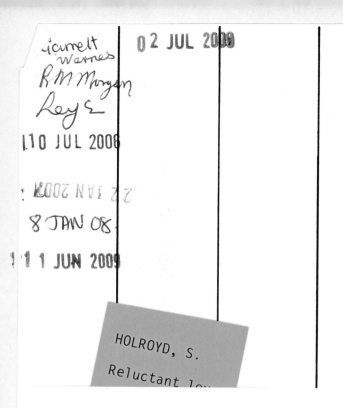